Adventures of Steve

Abir Gupta

First Printing: 2022

Copyright © 2022 **TDS Publication House**

All rights reserved.

ISBN: 978-93-94781-03-0

The Paperback Edition is in Black and White.
Printing & Distribution Rights: TDS Publication House, India.

Contents

Have Fun Reading.

CHAPTER 1

The Revenge of the Wither

The white sun shone down upon the village. Great oak trees danced in the light breeze as the grazing animals peacefully plodded along. Cheery villagers went about their lives, transporting hay bales, chopping down trees, and selling baked goods. The iron golem trudged around the village, observing the little children play happily in the multi-coloured field of flowers. It was a normal day in the village of Daint.

I'm Steve. I dwell in Daint, a small village in the countryside. I didn't always live here, though I was welcomed warmly into my new home. How I got here was a completely different story. I still remember it like yesterday. One stormy night, about a month ago, I went camping in the woods. I settled in for the night after a dinner of canned foods. I didn't know the time, but I knew it was late. Content with the world, I lay back in my sleeping bag. The moon was glistening like fairy dust. My heavy eyelids were closed within seconds. What seemed like a minute later, I was awake again. I couldn't tell any difference in time, but I knew something had changed.

Then I heard a rustle. A millisecond later, my cosy camp was blown into ruins. I had barely avoided the blast. Through the smoke, something stalked towards me.
Then I knew. One of the main dangers of camping in the forest. Mobs. I scrambled out of my tent.

Before I knew it, a horde of creepers was chasing me! Creepers didn't usually roam in packs but I guess they had their reasons. After a thousand miles of running, I spotted the warm lights of a village. What luck! I ran with all my might and plunged into the icy lake that lay between me and the village. As soon as I crossed the lake, I barricaded myself in the closest house to me. Its panelled floors gave me the impression that someone wealthy lived here. I relished the chance to catch my breath. But as they say, good times never last. I heard a foreboding hiss outside my house.

I tried to move, but I was paralyzed with fear. What happened next was a bit of a blur. I imagined half the house destroyed, chaos everywhere, and me, slumped against the flimsy table, unable to be saved. But that was not what happened. First, I heard an ear-splitting noise that was as loud as a volcanic eruption, then I saw just white and then just black.

CHAPTER 1.1

T he next thing I knew, I was staring at a thatched roof. Everything was a little blurry, so I closed my eyes. When I reopened them, I felt better and took everything I saw into account. I was in another house, but it was bigger than the one I hid in. I was lying on an aqua-coloured bed with silk sheets. There was a picture above me in a rusty bronze frame. It was of a creeper trampling on a farmer's crops. I mean, who would want to put up a picture like that?

And what a coincidence that creepers are now my least favourite mobs now (obviously)!

Suddenly, the front door opened. An elderly man walked in. He wore turquoise robes and had an impressive beard. He reminded me of a statue I saw at a castle of a legendary wizard. "Ah, good. You are awake." I didn't reply. I was wary of strangers. I think the man saw the suspicious look on my face because he said, "Don't fear. I won't hurt you. How do you feel?

"I'm fine," I replied a little more confidently. I felt comfortable now because I don't think he was going to attack me. Plus, how much damage can an old man do? (No offence to him.)

"So, what happened?" I asked.

"All in good time, child. First, eat this." the man replied. He handed me something gold and shiny. No way! It was a golden apple! They're almost as rare as emeralds!

I munched on it, satisfied. I felt a lot better and the apple washed out the fuzziness in my brain that I didn't realize was there. "Where did you get this?"

I enquired curiously. The man laughed. "So many questions!" I had a feeling that the man was stalling because we were reaching a touchy subject. Anybody would avoid talking about one of their neighbour's houses being blown up because of a reckless person like me. I was warned not to go camping alone but I can be stubborn...

"So, you want to know where I got this?" the man asked. "Our village has 2 main industries: farming and mining. Recently, we discovered a cave rich with gold ores. Then somebody had the bright idea of crafting the gold and apples together and we got this."

"That's cool!" I replied. Whoever thought of making these was a genius!

"Now I shall tell you what happened. A creeper blew up the house you were in and the rest of them came for you. But Toby spotted the chaos and rescued you before the creepers could blow again. I didn't know who Toby was but I was grateful to him.

The man called out to Toby, and a few seconds later, a man around my age walked inside. He had an iron sword in his hand, but his face was friendly. Toby wore light grey cargo trousers and a vibrant green and yellow top that said, 'I love Minecraft!'

"Hi!" he said, conversationally.

"Hi." I replied. Then I asked what was probably the most important question.

"Where even am I?"

"You are in the peaceful village of Daint. "I am the village elder." the old man told me. It looks like I just made two new friends!

CHAPTER 1.2

After I rested for another hour, Toby and the village elder took me on a tour of the village. Even though the village was small, there was a lot to see. There was a blacksmith, smoke pouring out of the chimney; the lake, full of exotic sea creatures; the apple farm, flourishing trees everywhere; and the armoury, the most exciting of them all. Rows of armour stood before me, ranging from leather to diamond. Every imaginable tool hung from the wall. Anvils sat in organised rows, and priceless ores filled dusty chests. In a second, smaller chamber, there was an enchanting table surrounded by many bookshelves. A middle-aged man with a bushy beard was enchanting two gold axes.
"Wow!" I said.

Soon after, we approached Toby's house, or what was left of it. A charred pit.

"I am so sorry," I told him.

"Don't worry. It was not your fault. "I thought I saw a flicker of hatred on his face, but within a second, he had returned to his usual self. Then something caught his eye in the wreckage. It was a singed diary. Most of its pages were black and the leather-cover had been burned away, but Toby still thought it was of use. As he flicked through the diary, I snuck a glance at it. There was some sort of sketch on one of the pages that looked like a flying skeleton with three heads. Below the drawing, I caught a glimpse of a few words: "Vivica reset-revive the Wither." I had no idea of what that meant, but I let it slip past me.

The picture was pretty intimidating but I thought Toby just liked drawing those kinds of things. Plus, I had to admit that it looked cool. Anyway, that had all been a month ago.

I'm getting used to living in Daint now. I've even built my own house. It's made out of birch wood planks and has a secret basement that is rigged with arrows and fire charges. Since the armoury was running out of space to put armour the village elder let me store the excess items in my basement. I have access to high-quality gear crafted from rare ores like diamonds. Since Toby didn't have a house anymore, I let him live with me to make up for it. I extended our house into one main room and two bedrooms. I think I did a pretty good job, if I had to say so myself!

I was pretty excited because the big bonfire was tonight. The whole village sat in front of a colossal bonfire and told each other stories. After that, we would have dinner together in the village hall. It was a village tradition that had been running for hundreds of years. However, we needed tons of wood for the bonfire, so we were sending out a couple of guys to collect dead wood from the forest.

Later that night, all the villagers gathered outside the sunflower field where we were igniting the bonfire. The orange glow of the sun cast a peaceful look on the village elder's face as he lit the bonfire and flamed it up into a fiery blaze, feeding it thick logs. Then he started telling us a truly extraordinary story. "Legend has it that over a thousand years ago, Daint was an entire kingdom ruled by King Alexander the Great. He was a good king and cared for his people well. However, from the depths of the underworld rose the Wither, a monstrous beast.

It attacked the kingdom and stormed the Overworld with its army of Wither skeletons."

"However, Alexander was not one to give up. He fought the Wither skeletons with his army and forced the Wither itself back into the Nether. At this point, Daint was in ruins. Over the years, Daint was rebuilt into this small but proud village. And that is how it's been ever since. "

Everybody started to clap. That was a pretty impressive story. But sometimes the past repeats itself, as I was about to find out how the hard way. Next, we had dinner in the hall. It was the best meal I have had in my life. There was every kind of food available in the Minecraft world!

I tried a bit of everything, and after my sampling, I felt like a plush toy that had been overstuffed. Then Toby walked towards me with a bowl of potato stew in his hand. "Try this; it's the best!" he said. "Okay, just a little!" I replied. The stew was as scrumptious as Toby described it.

I walked out of the hall feeling drowsy. After all that food, I was bound to feel tired... and sick. My tummy hurt. I know it was probably because I had eaten so much, but the stew that Toby had given me looked suspicious if you ask me.

Just to make sure, I went to the village elder. He told me to drink some milk to neutralise all poison effects. I felt better, but then I remembered something a potato farmer told me. She said that all of this village's crops were professionally cleaned, so the poisoned stew was no accident. It had been sabotaged! But by then, I was too sleepy to consider that so I just went to bed after a glass of hot milk.

CHAPTER 1.3

A few weeks later, an even more baffling incident occurred. The village elder asked me to accompany Toby on a mining expedition for some gold in the cave he told me about. I went to the armoury where Toby was waiting. He handed me an enchanted golden helmet. It glowed mystically in the lights of the armoury. "What is it enchanted with?" I asked.

"Protection II," he said. "C'mon."

After a twenty-minute walk through the sunflower plains, we arrived at the cave. It reminded me of a monster's open mouth with stalagmites and stalactites for fangs. The cave was dank, and bats flapped about. We placed a few torches around and got to work. I was sweating, so I took off my helmet; the inside was filled with sweat. It turns out that was a bad mistake.

All in all, we collected 34 gold ores all in all. Sweet! Even though it was hard work, the village elder promised to pay me in seeds, food and a hoe so I could start my own farm and breed animals. While I was left daydreaming of prosperity and riches, Toby had already reached the entrance of the cave. I stepped forward and felt myself sink a little into the ground. A pressure plate? Too late. The discreet line of Redstone glowed brightly and activated the TNT, which was hidden below the stone ground.

I ran towards the entrance where Toby was frantically beckoning me to get out. BOOM!

The TNT blew craters into the walls and floors, causing me to stumble as I sprinted to safety. The deafening explosions pushed me forward ruthlessly. Just as I thought the danger had gone, an entire chunk of stone came out from the ceiling and landed on my head. I wish I had my helmet! The cave swirled around me as I crumpled to the floor. The last thing I saw was the many tons of rock falling over me, trapping me in the dark abyss.

Just as it had been with the creeper, I woke up in the same bed in the same house. There was a bandage around my head. A few golden apples were piled up next to me. I reached out to take one and chewed on it absent-mindedly. I unsteadily got out of bed and walked towards the door. Toby came running towards me. "Hey, are you okay?" he asked worriedly. You look like you got pretty banged up!"

"Yeah, I'm fine." Toby and I sat at a table facing the setting sun. Then he said, "The cave collapsed after you got hit." I ran for help, and the iron golem broke through the rubble. It carried you home, where you were treated. However, the cave hadn't given in accidentally. The TNT was not an accident. Somebody wanted to hurt me desperately. I felt angry and confused at the same time. I didn't have any major enemies. I was about to ask Toby if he knew anything about who could be doing this, but I thought better of it. I didn't want to drag Toby into this.

CHAPTER 1.4

The next day, Toby showed me something spectacular. At about 5 'O clock, he said that he wanted me to follow him. We took an obscure route into the forest and walked for nearly an hour. "Are we there yet?" I asked, beads of sweat dripping from my head. "Nearly, just a bit more," he replied.

Soon after, we approached a clearing. Standing in the centre was a magnificent sight. A ruined Nether portal. Purple streams dripped down the ancient obsidian and the twisted trees covered its secret. Sizzling magma blocks surrounded it, set deep in the Netherrack where the portal sat. A small pool of lava sloshed about, behind the wonder. The one missing block of obsidian was nowhere to be seen. I reckoned erosion was common for a portal thousands of years old. Sitting next to it was a chest that was probably filled with loot. "Open it," Toby encouraged." I was waiting for you to see what was inside. I opened the chest without realising the red mark above the clasp. It was a trapped chest.

At least things can only get better. As soon as I opened the chest, I was blown backward into a tree stump. Toby cackled evilly. "Huh?" I was still too dazed to think properly. "You've fallen right into my trap!" Toby said. "What do you mean?" I asked. How could Toby be an enemy? "I'll tell you how!" he cried, as if he had read my mind.

"I was the one who planted the poisonous potato in your food." I rigged the cave with TNT. And now I'm going to destroy your village.

"But why?" I asked, bewildered. Toby's betrayal still hadn't hit me. "Why?" I repeated. "Because everything was perfect before you came along. The village loved me, but now they ignore me and adore their little hero. YOU!" he screamed.

And then he drew out his sword. "No. You wouldn't. "I said.

"Oh yes I will!" he bellowed and charged at me. I drew out my iron sword, but it was no match for his diamond tools. I barely had time to block his first blow. The impact cracked the edges of my sword. Toby was skilled—he didn't leave an opening for me. With one final slash, he disarmed me and shoved me back. I can't believe he betrayed me!

What he did next was even worse. He pulled out an obsidian block and a flint and steel. I knew what he was going to do before he did it. "NO!" I shouted, but it was too late. The Nether portal was alight. The skies turned grey. It started to rain. Thunder roared like a livid dragon. "Catch you later!" Toby smiled wickedly and fled into the forest. I called after him, but he was long gone. I just sat there rocking back and forth. Then I realised where I was and what just happened. I ran back to the village as quickly as my legs could carry me. We were in big trouble. I ran to the village elder's house and knocked hard. "Steve? What happened?" he asked. I rapidly explained. The village elder's face was pale and grave.

"We need fortifications. Arm each and every villager. I feared this day would come." He rang the bell. All the villagers approached us. "Prepare yourselves, for you are about to fight the biggest battle of your lives. Arm yourself with whatever is at hand. Fight with your lives!" The elder finished his pep talk and started handing out wooden, stone, and iron swords.

I dashed to the armoury and suited up with iron armour, a bow, shield, an iron sword, and golden apples. The diamond armour set was missing, and I think I knew where it went. Toby. When I got back outside, everyone was armed with swords or sticks. I even saw someone wielding a salmon! The fortifications were cobblestone towers with arrow launchers on top. There was also a moat filled with lava to keep Wither's skeletons out. The iron golem was ready to battle and punched through a block of cobblestone to test his strength. Then I heard the call of the Wither. The battle had begun.

CHAPTER 1.5

I can't write right now, so if there are no more pages, then we have lost and I have probably Withered away. First, the Wither was a black dot on the horizon. Then it was a smudge of dark grey, drawing closer. Finally, it was a three-headed beast shooting explosive skulls. First, it attacked a nearby house and blew the roof off. Then it stormed the barn and sent livestock running this way and that. "HEY! OVER HERE!" I called. The Wither turned to face me. It shrieked and flew at me at a terrific speed. I raised my shield and blocked the first skull. Instead of it bouncing off my shield, it exploded on impact.

I was thrown back viciously. A second skull came flying towards me. I yelped and dodged. I groaned and got to my feet. I loaded my bow and fired. It pinged harmlessly off the beast. It only enraged the Wither further. One arrow wouldn't do any harm, but lots of arrows might do the trick. I ran for the fortifications but then stopped as I was thrown back five blocks thanks to another Wither skull. We would never win at this rate! Then things got a lot worse. An army of Wither skeletons materialised in front of the village. They were regular skeletons but with stone swords and dark in colour. They were even more powerful than I described them. The villagers yelled and charged into battle. I heard the clinking of swords and the sound of pattering feet.

The iron golem was smashing through dozens of skeletons at a time, but he was slowly Withering away.

In the chaos, I made my way over to the fortifications and pelted arrow after arrow at the Wither. I could tell he was taking damage, but it wasn't enough. The Wither let out an ear-piercing shriek and shot a blue skull at me. Before I knew it, I was on the ground, the fortification was destroyed, and I was Withering away!

I quickly drank some milk and ate a golden apple and felt a lot better. Then the Wither went berserk and started shooting skulls everywhere. I ran into a house and cowered in a corner. BOOM! I was now sitting in a house that didn't exist. The damage was terrible and I knew I had to lead the Wither away. But first I needed its attention. There was a rattle. A Wither skeleton had snuck up behind me. It raised its sword, but I blocked it and kicked the mob into the iron golem's reach. I did not have time to finish it myself. I ran into the blacksmith and grabbed a piece of coal. It was the Wither's favourite food-supposedly. Praying it would work, I ran in front of the Wither.

It stopped screaming for a moment and considered me. Then it resumed its irritating sound and launched a skull at me. I blocked with my shield and smiled smugly. Then I looked down to see the horrific sight of splintered wood and a cracked handle. My shield broke! No way! I ran into the woods and realised that my best chance of defeating the Wither was to force it back into the portal. I hid behind trees, but the Wither seemed to have x-ray vision.

Soon, half the forest had gone up in smoke. "Almost there," I said to myself. I sprinted for the clearing with no cover. This was it: the finale.

The Wither tracked me down with ease, having a bird's eye view. I rapidly leaped to my left as the Wither shot at me with its skulls.

My armour protected me OK, but it would wear out eventually-then I would be a sitting duck.

I planned to make the Wither dive at me, then it would fly into the Nether portal. I positioned myself in front of the mystical structure. But instead of diving at me, it fired a blue skull at my chest. My faithful chest plate was destroyed, and I was thrown into the portal.

The Nether is one creepy place. Mounds of lava streamed down ancient cliffs. Various mobs prowled around. A lava lake ran across the place. Not pleasant. But the eeriest, craziest thing was the fortress that stood before me. It was made entirely out of Nether bricks and had an overall spooky atmosphere. And Toby was at the top of the fortress. He was sporting a diamond sword and a full set of diamond armour. I knew that the Wither would come for me, so I got a move on. I generated a new plan: lead the Wither into a dead end and just get out. I was lacking details, but it was the best plan I had. I figured out that the Nether fortress was as good as any place to trap it.

I jogged towards the foreboding structure. I didn't run because I would sweat and it was already hot enough down here. By "down here," I meant that the Nether was below bedrock. At first, I didn't believe it, but after seeing the endless bedrock ceiling, I thought better of it. I climbed up the mound of soul soil and entered the fortress. I saw many wonderful things, like a blaze spawner, and I stared at it for a moment before realising my stupidity.

A blaze rose from the miniature cage and started shooting fireballs at me! I loaded my bow and instinctively fired through the smoke.

I cheered as I heard the chink of the arrow embedding itself into the blaze.

I turned a few more corners before I heard footsteps. Toby! There was nowhere to hide. I turned to face him. "Steve! What a pleasant surprise!" Toby said in a sweet voice. Then his expression turned steely. He unsheathed his sword. I fired at him with my bow, but he deflected it with his weapon as if he was swatting away a fly. He laughed. "A disappointing performance!" he said, his voice tingling with amusement. "I haven't started yet." I charged at Toby and drew out my sword. We clashed. I slashed at him with an energetic feeling inside of me. But I was no match for him. Toby disarmed me and kicked me into a corner. He raised his sword and laughed. Finally! The pleasure of finishing you myself!" He raised his sword. I just sat there with my eyes closed. He had defeated me.

CHAPTER 1.6

I can't say I was glad that the Wither had followed me through the portal, but it saved me! At that precise moment, the Wither smashed through the wall, which made Toby turn around. I rapidly pushed him away and ran for it. I ran past another blaze spawner but didn't stop. I heard loud explosions behind me, which just made me run quicker. I burst out through the entrance. I thought I was going to make it easily, but I tripped in my over-confidence. In that split second, the Wither emerged from the fortress and spotted me. I ran faster than I had ever done before. I reached the edge of a cliff. There was the portal. My escape ticket was just five blocks away. I had come so close! But I wasn't giving up now. I took a run-up and leaped through the air. I probably wouldn't have made it, but the momentum from the Wither skull's blast helped me reach the other side.

Then I stopped as the Wither started to prepare its most powerful attack. A regular blue skull grew bigger and bigger. Then it started to crackle with electricity. I had to get out of there. I couldn't even dodge the colossal skull. I jumped into the portal at the same time the Wither launched the attack. The explosion was the loudest thing I had ever heard-louder than a creeper explosion! I had a faint memory of the Nether portal obliterated and me lying on the ground with my armour in ruins. I felt like I couldn't stand it. This was the end. Then I blacked out.

"I can't believe he survived that blast!" An unfamiliar voice drifted into my ear.

"Yeah, you could hear it from a mile away!" somebody said. My entire body ached, and I just wanted to sleep. I closed my eyes. I awoke again on yet another bed. This was the third time it happened! How embarrassing! But this time there was a small crowd gathered around me. "Hello?"Are you awake?" The village elder asked. "Steve?" I propped myself up on my elbows. Then the entire crowd swarmed me with their compliments and high-fives. "Now now, give the lad some space!" the village elder scolded. The crowd withdrew. "Now Steve, will you tell us what happened?" I explained. The crowd 'oohed' and 'aahed' when I reached an exciting point. "Quite an adventure!" the village elder remarked. "just like you, we have also won by defeating all the skeletons. Come with me."

The village had sustained a lot of damage and most of it was destroyed, but it was already being restored. "You saved the village, Steve. We are very grateful." Then everybody cheered and lifted me onto their shoulders, like in football matches. I felt glad that the Wither was defeated-well, sort of. I was also glad Toby had gone. I didn't know where he was, but I didn't care. I just had the biggest adventure of my life, and that was what mattered. The village was safe, and we had won. Victory!!!

CHAPTER 2

The Quest for The Totem of Undying

Hello again. I'm Steve, and this is my diary. I have previously written about the crazy adventure I had about six months ago. It involved Nether portals, boss mobs, betrayal, and action. We are now rebuilding our beloved village. The Wither was not one easy mob to defeat. But now it was trapped in the Nether- a place just as dark and deadly as the Wither itself. I continued placing oak planks down in the village hall. To be fair, this had all been my fault. I had put too much trust in Toby. I should have known his ulterior motives.

I continued my inspection and approached my house. My house hasn't suffered too badly, apart from that gaping hole in the wall that took out my framed photo of me sitting on the shore of the lake. Oh well. I could always get another picture. I had other things to worry about. I walked outside and surveyed the village. Everything was almost back to normal.

Apart from my favourite part of the village; the armoury. When I checked inside after the Wither's attack, most of the valuables were destroyed. The chamber full of enchanting books was destroyed. The arrow chest was destroyed. The armour stands were destroyed. Everything was destroyed!

And it's going to be a long time before we can restore the armoury to its former glory because where were we going to find more ores?

I decided to make this my mission. Replenish the armoury. I haven't had a stimulating, wholesome experience of mining yet, but I could do it. This was because the first cave I entered was rigged with TNT! Thanks to Toby. Toby was my former friend, but now he is my enemy. It turned out he was just trying to destroy Daint.

I desperately needed a friend, whether it was human or animal. I preferred animals because a pet dog or something like that wouldn't betray me and revive the Wither to take over the world!

At that moment, I heard a fearsome roar of pain coming from the woods. I was chased down by the Wither. If you're wondering what happened to the Nether portal in the woods, it was basically mined down block by block. It's gone now. But I got to keep the loot chest as a 'thank you" for saving the village. I haven't had a pleasant experience with the woods, either. I was betrayed by Toby in there and chased down by the Wither.

I ran into the forest and followed the roars of pain. There, struggling against vines, was the Iron Golem. He was bellowing and thrashing, trying to escape. Then he fell silent. I noticed a strange powder floating around next to him. Then I saw something even stranger. A peculiar flower was coughing out the powder onto the iron golem.

It was bright red in colour and its stem was spiked with thorns. I could tell it wasn't good for you because the golem's face was tinged green. I ran back home and got the village elder. The village elder was a tall man with a silvery beard. He was probably in his early sixties.

I found the elder sitting on a bench drinking coffee. "Hey," I said between pants for air. "The Iron Golem's in trouble!" The village elder rose to his feet. "Follow me," I said.

I lead the village elder to the iron golem. He bent down and ran his hand across the injured golem.

"He has encountered a mystical, dangerous plant," the village elder said, with his expertise in different types of herbs and fungi. "Only the Totem of undying will save him." Everybody gasped. I didn't know what the Totem of undying was. I would have known, but every book in the village has been destroyed and who knows what other useful things. "Somebody has to go find it," he continued. "A quest!" My eyes lit up with the prospect of another adventure. "I'll do it!" I said, excited.

"Then so be it." the village elder declared. "But the journey will be difficult..."

We spent the next day preparing for my adventure. The village elder told me everything about the totem. He said it was in a legendary lake that nobody had found before. Apparently, it was guarded by an army of one thousand drowned. How lovely. I took out my old iron armour and sword. I wish I had a shield, but the Wither destroyed it. Instead, I took an extra sword to keep in my offhand if the first broke. The village elder also handed me a piece of parchment with a faded line. It was a map. I also took some food with me.

Since the totem was in a lake, I needed a boat. I mined some wood and crafted my new mode of transport.

I was ready. Waving goodbye, I left Daint and headed South. The quest had begun. Trekking through the jungle was a lot harder than I thought it would be. I could only see a few metres ahead before the route was blocked by foliage. I had also bought a pair of shears to snip through the tree. They were doing their job well. A handy tool! After two hours of trudging through the jungle, I stopped for a break.

I took my heavy armour off and had an apple. Phew! It was hard work navigating a jungle. I suddenly realised that everything was bathed in a golden glow.

No way! It was almost night-time. I should have known that the sun sets quicker in places close to the equator. I hurriedly gathered some wood and started building. Then I noticed the mobs. Skeletons, spiders, zombies, you name it. No time to build a house. RUN! I slipped my armour on and ran through the trees. I heard the ping of arrows as the skeletons fired at me. As I ran, I noticed a cave. I was saved! if I reached the cave, I could block myself in and wait out the night. I successfully reached the cave and started to block myself in with wooden planks.

I sighed and placed a few torches around my makeshift home. It wasn't a five-star hotel, but it would do. I huddled in a corner and slept.

When I woke up, I knew I was in trouble. There was a hole in my wall, arrows in my armour, and my map was gone! The mobs must have broken through and stolen my map! I wasn't too worried about the mobs having the map because I'm pretty sure zombies and skeletons can't read.

Plus, the sunlight would have finished them off. Anyways, I was worried about how I was going to get to the totem without the map.

I remembered the map and pictured it in my head. I could roughly work out where to go, but it was a big risk. One little mistake and I could be off course for miles in this madness. I started off like the day before and made good progress. I scaled a tree to get a better vantage point and spotted a river half a kilometre away. I figured the river would lead me to the lake, so I decided to go there. I was about to climb down when the tree shook violently. I looked down and saw three creepers.

One creeper exploded, which made the tree fall. I leaped onto a branch of another tree and hung on. That tree crumbled to the ground as well. I thought my universe (Minecraft) defied physics! I landed on the ground with a thud. Falling from a tree was not much fun. The last creeper advanced toward me and was about to explode. I unsheathed my sword and unsteadily rose to the ground.

The creeper charged at me. I gripped the hilt of my sword tightly. Suddenly, a cat-like creature emerged from the trees. It hissed at the creeper, who backed away into the safety of the trees.

The animal turned to look at me. An ocelot?! No way! They were pretty rare! I stepped forward to stoke it. The jungle cat ran into the trees as fast as lightning. I chased after it. It soon reached the bank of the river I saw. "Ha! You're cornered! "I shouted. Then it jumped into the river. Seriously? I didn't know they could swim!

I was about to give up when I saw something glimmer in the water. Fish! If cats liked anything, then it was fish. I pulled out my fishing rod and swung it into the river. I reeled in a nice big salmon. The ocelot stopped in its tracks and stared at the catch. Then it jumped at me and snatched the fish off the floor. After its feast, it walked toward me and looked into my eyes. I had tamed an ocelot. I set my boat down on the water and got in.

The ocelot followed me on board. I didn't mind it because it was nice to have some company and it was so cute! I named it Shadow since it sneaked around in the darkness and didn't show itself until it came in front of the sun. We rowed down and knocked off ten miles of our journey. Satisfied, I stopped rowing. That's when I spotted the thing.

In the trees, I saw something tall and black with deep purple eyes.

Then it was gone. Tonight, We made camp under a colossal jungle tree. Shadow purred and lay down in front of the campfire. I put my back against the tree and got some sleep. I had a strange dream that I was being carried away by those strange black things again. They took me through the forest and turned a corner. That's when my dream ended. I awoke to the full moon and a black sky. It wasn't morning yet. I closed my eyes but opened them when a shadow squealed. I sat up and stared. Then I stared some more.
It was the black things. I remembered what they were called- Enderman. One of the Enderman noticed that I was awake and they started talking to me in incomprehensible squeals. Then it showed me the map.

I don't know the Enderman's language, but I could make out this: "If you help us, we will show you where the legendary lake is." They seemed to be nodding a lot, so I nodded as well, staring into their eyes. Oops!

The tallest Enderman started to angrily squeal at me and raise his hands, but the other Enderman refrained. "Don't stare at Enderman," they seemed to say. Well, at least I learned something new! The tallest Enderman, who I nicknamed Lofty, pulled out a small object. It was a square of flint and a steel rod. Flint and steel? Were they going to burn down the jungle? Then I saw the portal. The Nether portal. The portal to the place where the Wither was. NO! Lofty struck the two objects together and ignited the portal.

I braced myself for loud explosions and high-pitched shrieks, but none came. I stared into the portal.

There was a warped forest filled with huge warped fungi-a type of tree that grew in the Nether. The Wither was in another part of the Nether. I sighed with relief. But why did the Enderman need help? On that confusing note, they picked me up again and carried me into the portal.

This part of the Nether was different from the part I had visited earlier. Firstly, there were no mobs apart from the lazy Striders. Second, there was much more vegetation. The Enderman set me down on the floor and made sure that every Enderman had come through. They were about to pick me up again, but I held my hand up to stop them. I could walk perfectly fine on my own, thank you very much!

The Endermen took me to a cliff and pointed at something in the distance. I spotted a group of Piglin with ender pearls in their hands.

Lofty squealed. I worked out what he said. Stop the Piglin from stealing our ender pearls. I nodded because I didn't know how to respond. I wanted to help them, but I didn't know how. Before I could give that a thought, the Enderman linked arms and grabbed me. They were about to teleport. Teleporting is pretty unpleasant. At first, I felt like I was getting squeezed between two solid walls; then I thought I was being stretched like dough. But the experience lasted less than a second.

Purple particles floated around us as we warped near the Piglins. The Piglins got up and loaded their crossbows. They threatened to shoot when they saw the Enderman, but instead of fighting back, the Enderman teleported behind the pack of Piglin. Lofty gave me a small shove in the back, and I stepped closer to the brute.

The leader of the Piglins also stepped forward. I didn't have any training when it came to reasoning with Piglins.

"W-why are you stealing their ender pearls?" I enquired nervously. The leader (who I'm now calling Hammy) snorted and handed me a piece of paper. A Piglin diary? This was even crazier than my last adventure! I read, "Oink. Oink. Oink. Snort. Snort. Oink. Oink. Snort. OINK! How did Hammy expect me to understand this garbage? I handed him back his 'diary'.

I said, "Fine. Let's make a deal. If you give all their ender pearls back, then I'll reward you with some gold."

Hammy snorted and folded his arms. I saw the pile of gold behind him. It looked like this gold-loving mob had plenty of loot stashed up for himself. Then I remembered my golden apples. "How about this?" I asked. Hammy's eyes gleamed, and he lunged for the apple. I drew away. "The pearls first," I said. Hammy handed me back all of the Endermen's pearls eagerly.

I threw the apple as far as I could, and all the Piglins ran after it. Problem solved thanks to a bit of quick thinking! The Endermen swarmed me and lifted me up again as I gave them their pearls. They were chirping a lot, so I assumed they were saying their thanks.

We walked back to the portal in triumph. Then I smelled smoke. "Hey, is that-" I began. Whoomph! The forest was alight! I looked up and saw a Ghast. Its eyes were red, and it was shooting fireballs. So much for no mobs! The Enderman were teleporting everywhere, which is what they do when they're being attacked. I needed to think fast.

I grabbed an ender pearl that was randomly lying on the floor (possibly from a fallen Enderman) and threw it at the Ghast. I warped on top of the flying creature. The Ghast tried to throw me off, but I held on.

After a minute of being tossed about, I stuck my sword into the Ghast and jumped off as it disintegrated. Lofty called the Enderman back, and we got out of the Nether as fast as possible. I waved the Enderman goodbye as we set off for the Totem of undying. They chirped and vanished in a flash. Shadow and I walked to the edge of a cliff and peered down at the lake.

The Enderman told me where it was on our way back to the Overworld. It was still quite far off. You must be wondering how we got down the sheer cliff wall. Well, we didn't. We flew down. The Enderman had given me an elytra (a pair of wings) to help me on my quest. I swapped it for my chest plate and jumped with Shadow in my arms.

Flying is so fun! I glided down towards the ground like an eagle. The wind rushed past me as I soared through the air. I wish I was a bird! Shadow was actually quite light, so she didn't weigh me down. The ground was coming closer and closer... I knew how to fly but not how to land! I spotted a pond, so I dropped Shadow to make me more streamlined and nosedived into the water. SPLASH! I was sopping wet. Shadow, being a cat, didn't take any fall damage and licked me as I climbed out of the scummy pond.

Nice gift! I dried off and continued with my adventure. I was quite hungry, so I had a slice of melon which I found earlier. Shadow stalked off into the jungle to search for fish, so I was temporarily alone. I wandered around for a bit, waiting for Shadow to come back. Then I heard her calling for me. I followed the cries for help and reached a bog. Sitting on the shore was a witch's hut. Shadow was hanging from a tree in a net made out of biting wires.

I thought Shadow could squeeze herself out, but the gaps between the wires were as small as bottle caps. There was no escape.

I could cut her free, so I ran towards the net. But thanks to my stupidity, I got caught too. As I was running, my foot snagged on a tripwire and I was hoisted up into the air.

I groaned. What had I done? A witch came outside to see what all the commotion was. "Haha!" the witch cackled. "two catches in one day!"

"Let us go!" I shouted, furious.

"I don't think so!" The witch walked toward me and dropped a splash potion on the ground. I suddenly felt very tired. My eyelids were like lead, so I closed them. I awoke to the hiss of a cauldron as it boiled water. The witch was throwing potions inside the cauldron, muttering to herself, "It's nearly done! Soon I will have control over every mob in this world and I will rule the world. I didn't exactly understand what she meant, but I didn't think much of it.

I was trapped in a cage with Shadow. Luckily, Shadow was thin enough to slip through the bars of the cage. I pointed at the keys, and she sneaked over to them. Shadow picked them up with her mouth and came back. I secretly unlocked the door and sneaked out. Then, I stepped on a creaky floorboard. Creek! The witch turned around. "What-how did you?" she stammered. I took the opportunity to kick her cauldron to the floor, causing the contents to spill out. "NO!" she cried. "This will set me and my plan back for weeks!" She narrowed her eyes and glared at me. Shadow bared her teeth and I readied my pickaxe. (My sword was leaning on the wall on the other side of the room.) The witch pulled out a potion.

"Another time!" She said, and dropped the potion. The room filled with smoke. My eyes stung badly. When the smoke cleared, the witch was gone. She had got away.

I took a look around the room. Was there anything useful that I could pinch? I checked the brewing stand and there was a Nether wart, blaze powder, and a water bottle. I could make a potion of strength! I mixed the three substances and bottled my potion. This would help me battle the drowned. I and Shadow set off again after a quick snack. It wasn't far now. After half an hour of walking, we reached our destination. The Legendary Lake!

The water was crystal-clear and many exotic fish swam beneath the water. Towering trees bordered the lake like guardians. Beautiful flowers grew on the banks like moss in the rain. It was a heavenly sight. And there, on a stone pedestal, was the Totem of undying. There it was! The reason we had gone through so much trouble. The reason we crossed a whole jungle. The reason we had this grand adventure. I placed my boat down and rowed through the lake. As I reached the tiny island in the middle of the lake, all the jungle noises stopped. The birds weren't chirping. The fish weren't splashing.

The sun intensified its merciless glare. I reached out to take the totem. As soon as I touched the life-saver, the ground shook. The pedestal sank into the ground, taking the totem with it.

"What?" I exclaimed. Splash! I and Shadow turned around. Hundreds of Drowned emerged from the lake, wielding tridents. They all swam towards me. Oh no! I pulled out my spare sword. Shadow's claws scratched at the ground. We were strong, but I didn't think a person with only iron sword, and a pet ocelot could defeat one thousand drowned.

The drowned were basically under-water zombies who couldn't stand the sun like regular zombies. Unfortunately, the sun had just disappeared behind the rolling hills. We had to fight.

The first drowned raised its trident and threw it at Shadow. She tried to escape, but her tail was pinned by the trident. Shadow mewed in pain. I swung my sword at the drowned and it fell into the water. Only 999 to go! There wasn't much room on my tiny strip of land, so I didn't have enough space to dodge. The drowned that came near the island was toast, but the rest of them were smart. They stayed back and aimed at me with their weapons.

I ducked a few, but one of the tridents caught me on the shoulder. I pulled it out, but it still hurt badly. Now I was practically useless because my sword-fighting arm was injured. There was no way I could win! At precisely that moment, a burst of light erupted from behind me. A Nether portal?! This could only mean one thing.

Swarms of Enderman and Piglin stepped out of the portal. Lofty and Hammy were leading their parties through the portal. The Piglin wore gold armour and were equipped with crossbows and swords. The Enderman wielded Netherrack blocks. They all charged into battle, leaving me and Shadow in the dust. Some Endermen teleported to the bank and some stayed to protect us. Since they were allergic to water, the Enderman didn't enter the lake. The Piglin, on the other hand, charged through the water and fired with their crossbows. I saw one Piglin who spotted another ocelot and started chasing it. Well, good luck with that!

They weren't very smart, but they were good fighters. Lofty and the other Endermen teleported everywhere to confuse the drowned and then attacked with their blocks.

The Drowned marked them down with their tridents, but the Enderman teleported to safety. Meanwhile, I was attending to Shadow. I pulled the trident out of her tail and got some bandages out. I bandaged her tail up and gave her a raw salmon to distract her from the pain.

Finally, the Endermen and Piglin were able to force the remaining drowned back into the water. They wouldn't rise again anytime soon! I thanked both the Endermen and Piglin. The only thing left was the totem. I explained what happened to the mobs. They pointed at the hole and nodded. I guess they wanted me to get the totem. I peered down at the hole. I couldn't see the bottom. There was only one thing for it. I had to jump. Looking back, I should have teleported with an Enderman, but it didn't matter. I took a deep breath and jumped.

The hole probably went down at least 30 blocks. Luckily, there was a deep puddle at the bottom. I placed some torches and took in my surroundings. Damp walls surrounded me, and there was a minecart on a rail. I stepped in and pulled the lever. The minecart began to move forward. Behind me, I heard the walls collapse. No escape. I willed the minecart to go on. I saw creepers hidden in the rough cave walls and spider webs filling up the nooks and crannies. I felt very hot for some reason.. Soon I came to a bridge and knew why. There was a massive pit filled with lava! I pulled sharply on the edge of the cart, and it skidded off the track.

I picked myself up and inspected the bridge. It had lots of gaps in it and didn't look very strong. I tested it by tapping my foot on the first plank. The entire bridge gave away and sank into the lava.

"That was a close one!" I bridged across with dirt blocks and reached the other side. I was dripping with sweat, having crossed over lava only a few metres below me. I walked on. After a few minutes, I approached a dead end. No!

I calmed myself down and looked at the walls. One section seemed to be painted. I pressed my hand against it and it flipped open. A hidden chamber! Wow! I walked into the room, sword in hand. I saw the totem sitting on the same pedestal. Yes! The confusing part was how it got here. But again, if evading death, by holding a fancy object in your hands was possible, then this was possible. I had completed my quest! Or not. I heard footsteps behind me. A familiar person walked into the chamber. I hadn't closed the door! My arch-enemy Toby, laughed. "How nice of you to leave the door open!" he chortled happily.

"Toby," What are you, of all people, doing here? I asked. "If you were smart, which you obviously aren't, then you would know I couldn't let this once-in-a-lifetime opportunity slip."

"How did you get in?" I enquired. How had he gotten past the Enderman and Piglin? "There's something called a shovel, you know! Anyway, out of my way. You don't deserve the totem!" he bellowed.

"Well, neither do you." I retorted. "Now let's end this." I thought it was a good time to drink my potion, so I took a swig from the glass vial. Then I gripped my sword and charged. Toby and I clashed. He had a diamond sword but no armor, so I could easily win if he left an opening. On the other hand, my injured arm held me back. Toby easily disarmed me and sent me flying away from the totem with a shove. "HA!" "The totem is mine!" he declared with glee.

"NO!" I called. But, as soon as Toby touched the totem, the cave rumbled.

Huge chunks of rock dislodged themselves from the wall and fell around us. In the chaos, I grabbed the totem of its plinth and ran for it. The hidden chamber's ceiling gave away completely and buried the room under boulders. The rest of the cave was also collapsing, so I got out of there as quickly as I could. I went past my adapted bridge, past the blocked exit (which I hurriedly mined out), and came to a stop at the drop. I had to climb. I jammed my pickaxe into the wall and pulled myself up.

My limbs ached with pain, but I had nearly reached the top. Just as soon as I thought I was safe, my foot got caught in a wedge as the walls collapsed. I was pretty much out of the cave apart from my foot. All the Endermen and Piglin pulled with all their might. They finally wrenched my foot out between. I lay, exhausted, on the ground. I didn't look too good. My shirt was torn in places, dust covered my face, and my ankle was swollen. Shadow licked me lovingly. I stroked her. Then I said to the Enderman and Piglin, "Thank you so much."

"I couldn't have done this without you." The Piglin snorted, but Lofty's reply was clear in my head. 'I will miss you!' He just used telepathy!

"I'll miss you too." I said sadly. "um- could you do me one last favour?" I waved to the Piglin as the Enderman transported me home. Then, after one happy Vvoop, they vanished.

It was night in the village. I grasped the totem and knocked on the village elder's door. His eyes widened as he opened it. "Steve! You are back! "And you bought a friend!" he smiled at Shadow. Did you get the totem?" I nodded. The elder beckoned me inside. The iron golem was lying on a mattress on the floor.

I passed the totem to the elder, who placed it in the iron golem's blocky, massive hands. We waited for a heart-stopping moment. The totem began to glow. Was it working? The iron golem slowly opened his eyes. Then he got up, fit as a fiddle. He stared at the totem as it disappeared in a burst of vivid green. Then he stared at me.

The iron golem gave me a pat on the back, which hurt a lot more than I thought it would. It was basically getting punched by a block of steel, which doesn't sound very nice. The village elder congratulated me. "Steve, you have saved our village protector. Thank you! Now, shall we heal your cuts and bruises? "The village elder cleaned my shoulder wound and bandaged my foot. I then had a bath and changed into a fresh set of clothes. We had a big party, after which I told everyone about my epic adventure! I couldn't be happier.

The iron golem was safe, I had a pet ocelot, and Toby was defeated! For now, that is. But I wasn't going to waste my time thinking about him. I was a hero. So, that's the end. I really didn't expect another adventure, but it was certainly one I wouldn't forget in my lifetime!

CHAPTER 3

The Lost Letter

It all started when the mobs came. They spawned due to unknown reasons and invaded our village. There was no option. We had to leave.

Clink! I wiped my brow. Phew! Mining was hard work. I raised my pickaxe and embedded it into a large boulder, which split open to reveal a vein of diamonds. 1, 2, 3, 4, 5-diamonds! The mine of the day! I hadn't really mined anything else apart from a bit of coal, so I was content with my find. I mined a bit more to see if there were any more diamonds, but I came up empty-handed. Oh well! Five diamonds were enough for a diamond helmet! The people at the armoury were going to love these!

I have just returned from another crazy adventure. Our iron golem was seriously ill, so I volunteered to search for the totem if undying to revive him. I found the totem, an ocelot who is now my pet and a whole host of trouble. But I returned in one piece (more or less) and healed the iron golem.

So, I returned to my current focus: mining. Almost a year ago, the dreaded Wither attacked our village. The armoury sustained a great loss. Plus, we lost our diamond armour, not because of the Wither but something even worse. Toby, My former friend, now my enemy. He was just trying to destroy our village and rule the world.

I shuddered thinking about the last time I clashed with him. Even with a strength potion, Toby was still stronger than me.

Maybe because he had a diamond sword, but to be fair, he stole it, not crafted it from his own hard work.

Perhaps I needed to work on my fighting skills too. Anyways, this cave was discovered recently, and now we have hundreds of miners labouring down here. It might seem like hard work (which it is), but it is also quite fun. I bagged my loot and hopped on a rickety minecart. This was a new system in the cave which helped us miners get around the place a lot quicker. We were also transported to our homes directly from the cave. As I passed through the eerie cave, I spotted creepers peeking through holes in the wall. Creepers aren't really that bad down here. In fact, they're quite helpful. Every once in a while, the creepers chase down miners and explode. Their explosions open up whole new networks of caves. They are just as efficient as TNT. Maybe a little more dangerous, considering TNT doesn't chase you around and explode without warning.

I pulled on the rusty lever and the minecart grinded to a stop. I entered a built-in checkout. I handed the cashier my bag of loot. "Wow, Steve, nice find!" he said, impressed. Then he reached into the bag and handed me two of the diamonds. "This is your pay for the day. Good job!" Two diamonds! The cashier was really generous. I could craft a diamond sword with this stuff!

"Thanks!" I replied happily. Then I got onto the minecart and headed home.

Mobs were peeking out behind the trees, so it must be evening. Time passed pretty quickly in the caves! I entered my humble home. Shadow, my pet ocelot, was waiting at the door. I stroked her before heading to my crafting table and crafting a diamond sword. It was amazing!

I went outside to test it. I saw a zombie randomly walking about, so I swung my sword at it. Slice!

The zombie fell to the ground. Wow, this was so efficient! It's probably why Toby was so strong! I went back inside and washed my hands. Time to cook! I was pretty hungry, so I made quite the feast. Plates of chicken lined the table, surrounded by loaves of bread, with melting cheese dripping down the sides. Baked potatoes sat on sparkling plates next to bright orange carrots swimming in melted butter. I gave Shadow some salmon for dinner, which is her favourite.

Flash! Huh? I glanced at the window. A thunderstorm! The first one this year! It must be my lucky day! I just wish I knew how wrong I was. I sat at the table and dug in. Mmmm! Scrumptious! I knew that I couldn't finish it all, so I stored away the leftovers for later in a chest. I had nearly finished my meal when I heard the groans. Was my tummy still hungry? Shadow was squealing at the window. I peered up. Then I looked down at Shadow. It couldn't be. I checked again to make sure it wasn't an illusion. Nope. There they were, masses of zombies, creepers, and skeletons staring at us through the window.

What! How on earth did so many spawn? The crowd of mobs slowly dispersed. Phew! I sighed and sat at the table. Shadow was still shivering. "Hey, it's OK. The-"I started.

Boom! The mobs poured into my house, climbing through a hole that had appeared from thin air. I narrowed my eyes. The only thing that could have done that was a creeper. The skeletons loaded their bows and I came to my senses. We had to get out.

There was something strange about the mobs. For some odd reason, all their eyes were a deep shade of purple like they were hypnotized... I grabbed my pickaxe from my item frame and opened the trapdoor to my basement.

"Shadow, get in!" I shouted. Shadow and I climbed down the ladder and shut the trapdoor. I sighed again. What just happened? And was the rest of the village safe? I remembered the village elder. He was old and vulnerable. Hopefully, the iron golem would protect everyone. He could handle a few skeletons, right?

Shadow mewed. I looked up only to see a creeper jumping on the trapdoor. Soon it would explode. I needed to think fast. The only tools I had were a sword and a pickaxe, which wasn't great for fighting. But it was good for mining. I could dig an escape tunnel! I thought about taking down the mobs with my sword, but I would be swarmed. Plus, I had no protection. I used to have armour down here, but we moved it back to the armoury. But I kept my precious gold helmet, which I wear every day at the mine.

I wore that helmet when I first went mining. It was a successful day if you don't count the TNT, getting knocked out, and being dug out by the iron golem. Anyway, I calculated that I needed to mine about twenty metres in the correct direction.

I could escape the village then and get help. As I was mining, I heard the distinctive sound of a creeper exploding. "Oh no!" They had broken into the basement! I mined faster, urged on by Shadow. Meanwhile, a zombie had just moved a single inch towards us.

Soon we mined our way outside. In my panic, I didn't realise that I had mined into a large hill. I stepped forward onto thin air. Whoops! I picked myself up. I was standing on soggy grass. I looked up and saw that I was lucky to have survived a fall from that height. Twang! An arrow landed next to me. "You have got to be kidding me!" I said out loud. Couldn't the skeletons give me a break?

It turns out skeletons weren't the only danger. A phantom knocked into me, sending me flying to the ground. Every time I stood up again, I would be on the ground within a second. The phantoms were just too fast! I pulled my sword out and tried to hit them, but I missed every shot. On top of that, the skeletons were still shooting at me.

I thought I was done when I heard a voice shouting, "Stop!" My mysterious saviour was holding an iron axe. He strode forward and attacked. I tried to pick myself up, but I had no energy. Sleepiness took over me like a tsunami.

I woke up in an old bungalow. I was sleeping in a green bedroll. I thought it was all a bad dream, but I saw the same iron axe propped up against the wall.

Shadow was next to me, sleeping deeply. I got up and left the room. An old but strong man was making sandwiches in the kitchen. I cleared my throat to get his attention.

"Hmm? Oh, it's you!" "He said in a surprised tone. "didn't fancy seeing you here this early!"

The man, who was called Dave, told me about himself. He was a lumberjack who collected wood for a living. He asked me where I came from, and I replied, "Daint."

"Oh, so you escaped?" Dave handed me a newspaper. It said: 'A small village in the north was attacked last night. Hundreds of mobs swarmed the place; it was too dangerous for anybody to escape. Experts assume that the storm nicknamed "Darren" had something to do with the strange appearance of so many mobs together.

Then the paper rattled on about how storms could power up mobs like charged creepers. There was nothing else to do with my village.

"I'm going back right now," I said defiantly. Shadow had just woken up and was chewing the newspaper. "No! That's insane!" Dave shouted. "You could never take on the mobs alone! Your destination is Axeblade. "Axeblade is a large city not far from Daint. Dave said I should ask the king for help. "Ok. We'll go to Axeblade," I replied obediently. It was better than going back to an abandoned village full of dangerous creatures. We would leave the next day, at the crack of dawn.

For breakfast, Dave gave me a couple of cheese and pickle sandwiches to have for breakfast.. He had a can of tuna for Shadow. Dave waited for me to finish and then asked if I wanted to help him cut down some trees down. I agreed readily. It would be a brand-new experience.

"Here" Dave handed me an iron axe. We worked all day until we had a decent pile of birch wood.

I asked what he did with the wood after he'd finished, and he said that the wood was given to Axeblade for construction work.

Dave had a very important job if he was supplying vital building materials to one of the biggest cities in Minecraft! "Well, I think that's enough work for today!" Dave panted. "Let's have dinner!"

We had dinner in the kitchen. It wasn't as grand as the dinner I had the day before, but it was still good. Dave had made a pumpkin pie, accompanied by a generous helping of sweet berries. After dinner, I followed Dave outside onto the porch. "Dave, thanks for all your help. I really appreciate it.

I told him "If there's anything that I can do to help-"
"Steve, it's OK," he said a little forcefully. "actually, there is something you can do." I was glad that I could repay Dave.

"In Axeblade, there is a young lady called Alex. When you find her, can you give her this letter?" He handed me a parchment that was yellowing with age. "I promise I will get this to her," I said. It was the least I could do for Dave. "Thank you, Steve."

The next day, I woke up as early as possible. It was time to go! I woke Shadow up and then gathered some resources. I took some food, torches, and Dave's good luck.

After a quick bite for breakfast, I headed out. "Bye!" I waved at Dave happily. He had helped me so much!

"Farewell, Steve! One day, we will meet again!" He shouted from his porch. Then he went inside and walked out of sight. I and Shadow walked through the forest. It was different from the jungle since the trees weren't packed together and it wasn't humid and impenetrable.

Soon, we approached a sign. It said, Axeblade 10 miles East.'

Great! We had nearly reached our destination. The sun set as soon as it rose. We were only a few miles away from Axeblade now so I didn't worry too much. I didn't want to waste time making a shelter, so I just slept under a large oak tree. Groan. I opened my eyes. There were mobs surrounding me everywhere. Shadow fled into the trees, but I pulled my diamond sword out. Time to fight.

I walked through the hoard of mobs and beckoned them towards me. They slowly moved forward. They moved forward towards their end.

I slashed and sliced with my sword. Most of the mobs swarmed me, only to fall at my feet. The creepers did more damage to the zombies and skeletons than to me. I could do this.
But every time I thought they were all gone, the relentless mobs re-emerged from the trees once again. I knew I couldn't handle all of them, so I retreated into the woods. The mobs, however, were smart. They cornered me and began to close in.

I stepped backward onto a pile of leaves that immediately gave away. I fell into the darkness.

I caught glimpses of what was going on. Two men in leather armour walked toward me. The next thing I saw was the stone ceiling of a castle. I finally awoke to the smirking face that belonged to Toby. He was wearing a golden crown studded with diamonds and emeralds. I don't know what the odds are of running into evil masterminds again and again, but this was ridiculous!

I was chained to a wooden chair. "Let me go!" I shouted furiously. I needed to get away from this place. "I don't think so!" Toby laughed. "guards, chuck him in cell number three, NOW!" The guards unchained me from the chair and roughly shoved me into a dingy dungeon. Then I heard one of them lock the door shut, followed by a little splash. They had chucked the keys into the sewers! I'll get you, Toby, I thought. Even if it's the last thing I do!

Then I realised I couldn't do anything. I was trapped in an inescapable dungeon filled with spiders. I would never see Shadow again. I couldn't save Daint. And most importantly, I couldn't deliver the letter to Alex. "It's over!"

I shrieked, but nobody could hear me. In anger, I threw the letter into the darkness. Then the most mysterious thing happened. The letter came flying back to me. "It's not over." said a voice. "Huh? Who's there? "I asked worriedly. A woman with ginger hair emerged from the shadows. "I'm Alex and we can get out of this. What's your name?" Alex? It couldn't be!

"Steve." Then I added, "A-Alex? I have something for you." I handed her the letter. She read," Dear Alex, I am writing to say hello. How are you?
I hope you enjoy your time in Axeblade. Remember, don't come looking for me because the forest is too dangerous. We will meet again one day. From, father."

Dave was Alex's father?! This was getting slightly confusing. Alex rolled up the letter and slipped it into her belt. "Thanks, Steve. Now, let's escape and meet my father again!" Alex led me to one side of the dungeon where a solitary torch was flickering in the darkness.

"I've been using my daily water supply from the guards to weaken the walls of the dungeon. Since the building material isn't very strong, the wall should crumble. Eventually, that is." Have you got any water, by the way? I'm pretty thirsty!"

I handed Alex my little bag made out of deerskin. She took a swig from the bottle. Then I asked "How did you get stuck in here?"

"I was captured. You see, I wasn't born here. I moved to Axeblade just before a big battle. The king thought I was a spy for the enemies so he imprisoned me. One day, I will have my revenge." Alex finished her speech, but I still had one more important question.

"Do you know anything about the king?" I enquired. Alex sighed. "I'm afraid that I know a lot more about the king than I wanted to. The so-called king is actually Herobrine. He is basically an evil incarnation.

He wants to rule the world and destroy all small communities to make way for a massive one ruled by him."

Whoa, I thought. Toby-I mean Herobrine is pretty ambitious (Though he should have thought of a better pseudo than Toby!)

"So, what do we do now?" I spoke. All this information was useful, but how could we defeat Herobrine ourselves? "What do you mean? We escape and then take down Herobrine." Alex said. I shook my head slowly. It's not that simple! Herobrine is really strong! "I retorted.

Alex ignored me and fingered the damp wall. She was about to add more water when the wall blew wide open. Standing in the smoke was an indistinguishable figure. He was young, had short brown hair, and was wearing iron armour. "Jay?" Alex seemed surprised. Jay-whoever he was-clambered through the hole and said, "TNT. Now come on."

Alex, me, and Jay ran through the narrow passages. "Why did you help us?" Alex asked. Jay replied but didn't stop running.
"I know of the king's plans. Since Axeblade isn't safe anymore because of Herobrine, I decided to gather up as many people as possible and get out. Who's that?"

Alex replied, "Steve. Steve, Jay. Jay, Steve." I was about to ask another question, but I figured we could talk about the minor details after escaping the castle and getting back to Dave. As we turned another corner, I knew we were in big trouble.

Herobrine laughed his cruel, mirthless laugh. "My, quite an impressive escape! No matter, everything ends NOW! " He drew out his diamond sword. Jay loaded his crossbow, and Alex pulled out a cracked stone sword. I, on the other hand, had no weapons on me, so I readied my fists. Then we fought. Herobrine deflected Jay's shots and blocked Alex's sword.

I punched him in the stomach, which made him stagger back. I took the opportunity to kick him to the floor and grab his sword.

"Great!" cheered Jay. "but we need to get out of here fast because I, the Redstone master, rigged the castle with TNT, which is set to explode in-" He checked his watch. "two minutes!" We dashed out of the castle but screeched to a halt when I spotted Shadow slinking into the castle. "No!" I shouted and ran after her. I couldn't just leave her with about five hundred TNTs!

"STEVE!"Steve! Wait!" Alex and Jay bellowed from the outskirts of the forest. I pretended not to hear them. I needed to save Shadow. I saw a group of guards raise an alarm, and they began to chase me. I finally found Shadow nosing through some tins of tuna in the kitchen.
Seriously? "Shadow, come on!" I hissed. Shadow ignored me, but I pocketed a can of tuna to make her follow me.

There were probably about thirty seconds left to escape the castle. I reached the courtyard and thought I was going to make it, but then Herobrine popped out of nowhere! "You're not going anywhere!" he declared.

I knew Herobrine was our enemy, but I had to tell him about the TNT if I was to get out safely.

"Look, the entire castle is set to blow! If you don't let me go, then it's the end of both of us!" I said frantically. Unfortunately, Herobrine was not giving in. "LIES!" he shrieked and charged at me. I slid to avoid the attack and continued through the courtyard. But it was too late. The explosions had begun.
They started underground in the dungeons, which toppled the foundations of the castle. A towering column of marble was poised to fall on me. I was doomed.

I couldn't move. I was paralysed by fear, like I had been so many times before. Shadow had already moved out of harm's way, but my muscles seemed to have jammed up. The column was slowly toppling forward when Alex pushed me out of the way. She took the fatal blow instead. "ALEX!" I screamed. I tried to lift the massive marble column, but it was just too heavy.

Jay ran forward to help. With our combined strength, we managed to lift the pillar off Alex. Thankfully, she was okay. Alex had mined down a few blocks to avoid getting crushed. Shadow licked her happily. Alex climbed out of the hole she had mined. She was smiling, but her expression quickly changed to a look of alarm. A flaming arrow whizzed through the smoke, setting fire to the planks of wood around us. I thought I saw a figure in the distance wearing a crown watching us.

I tried to call after Herobrine, but he disappeared. Jay, Alex, and I needed to get back to Dave. Everybody had abandoned Axeblade because of the 'castle siege'.

We ran into the forest before anyone could come and investigate. Shadow had rejoined us and was stalking through the treetops. After an hour of limping through the dense woods, we called it a day. I rested on a rock to heal myself up from the damage I had taken during my fall the day before, while Jay and Alex went to fetch wood for a campfire.

What a day! We had been locked in a dungeon, fought Herobrine, and escaped a TNT-loaded castle. All we had to do now was to get back home. Speaking of home, I don't even know if I can return to Daint. But there was no harm in checking if the village was up and running.

Soon, Jay and Alex returned. We lit the campfire and nibbled on wild berries. Then Jay started talking. "Steve, let me tell you how I know Alex and why I helped you," he began. "it all started when I joined the king's army. Herobrine ordered me to arrest Alex and I refused. But Alex didn't know that I had been forced to imprison her, so she thought I was an enemy. I knew it was too dangerous to break her out, but I finally found the proof that made me do it. I saw Herobrine hunched over a map, crossing out neighbouring kingdoms. Next to each cross, he wrote: to be obliterated. So yeah. What's your story?

I told them about my many adventures, how I met Shadow, fought the Wither, and went to the Nether. "Wow, that's quite an adventure!" remarked Alex. We chatted for a bit more before turning in for the night.

I had a strange dream and guess what? Herobrine was in it. I dreamt that he had survived the downfall of the castle and was muttering to himself, "That's it.

I have to release the ender dragon. "I didn't make much sense of what I heard, but I didn't really care since it was just a dream. Or was it?

I had completely forgotten about my peculiar dream and the four of us continued on our short journey. I was very worried about the village because I didn't think we could return to live there. But as I said, we have to check it out.
We walked in silence until we approached the oak sign, which said, Axeblade-10 miles. We were excited because both Alex and I knew we were close to home. "Nearly there!" she exclaimed. After an hour of walking, we reached the hut. Alex was really excited and she knocked on the door, but no answer came. Confused, she entered her former house with me and Jay following close behind.

Everything was how Dave left it, but he wasn't there. Perhaps he had gone off to chop some trees down? Shadow and I checked out the familiar forest, but we found nothing. After thinking about giving up, Jay called for us from inside the cottage. Alex and I ran in and joined Jay, who was huddled around the bedside table.

There was a note. I picked it up and read, I have taken your Dave to a place where you will never find him. But, if you want Dave back, then you must come to rescue him from the End. Steve, Alex, and Jay, if you don't come within a fortnight, then Dave is dragon chow. From Herobrine. I can't believe he would do this! Alex looked heartbroken. She pocketed the note and spoke quite calmly, considering the circumstances. "We go back to Daint, then work on getting to the end.

We have two weeks, which is practically no time at all to get to the End. "Let's go!" she added fiercely.

We hurried back to my home. When we got there, the whole place was deserted. A couple of zombies in leather caps roamed around. The crops were trampled. Everything was grey and gloomy. We searched around for a few hours, but we found no one. I couldn't think of anywhere else to look apart from the caves, so that's where we went. It was obvious that no one was there, so we trudged out sadly.

But everything changed when I entered my house. Things were not normal. At least the basement wasn't. When I entered the basement, it was crammed with villagers. This is where they had been all along! My tunnel had been blocked off, but the rest of my basement had been enlarged. I scanned the crowd for the village elder and there he was! I didn't think I would be seeing him again! By now, all the other villagers had stopped in their tracks as they noticed me.

All of them assaulted me with questions as I ran over to the elder. He was in deep conversation with another woman. "Yes, the witch of the South is..." he stopped and stared at me. "Steve?! "You are alright!" the elder exclaimed. We thought you were gone forever-who are they?" He pointed at Alex and Jay.

I sat down on a chair. I had a whole bunch of explaining to do. After I enlightened the elder about everything from the forest mobs to finding the note on the table, I asked a question of my own. "Is everyone here alright?" The village elder sighed.

"We came to your house for help, but you had disappeared."

We coped well, apart from losing a few of our people. "I instantly felt a pang of guilt. I should have been here to help my friends... "I sent a spy to tell us about the current situation." One day, I was informed about the witch of the South. She hails from the jungle.

The jungle? Could this be the very same witch who imprisoned me and Shadow? "She mind-controlled all of the hostile mobs in the vicinity and attacked us.
A few days after I heard of this witch, we met her in person. She said that she wanted somebody. And that somebody was you."

I knew it! It was that very same witch I had met not so long ago. I told the village elder about this and offered to help. "Hmmm. That would be appreciated, Steve, but you need to help Dave and get him out of the End," he said. Alex looked worried when he mentioned Dave. "Don't worry; we'll defeat the witch. Who said we can't do both? "I looked over at Alex to see if she approved. If she wanted to rescue Dave, then that's what we were going to do.

Alex gave me a little nod. She said, "Protecting the village is our priority." We are skilled enough to rescue my father after saving the village. Let's do this. "Jay seemed ready too. I turned back to the elder, who had a shadow of doubt on his face but quickly changed his tune. "Then so be. The witch is going down."

CHAPTER 4

War For Daint

Place another arrow dispenser right there! I called. We needed as much protection as possible. In case you're wondering why we need protection, the Witch of the South invaded our village. She's coming back every other night with her hypnotised mobs, so we have less than two days to prepare our defences. Even though there's a lot to do, things are running smoothly thanks to Alex and Jay, my two best friends. My pet ocelot, Shadow, was staring at me through my house window. I didn't let her out because we were experimenting with arrows. She didn't really need one stuck in her tail!

I was working on the arrow dispensers. Basically, a mob would activate the cleverly-placed tripwire, which would send a Redstone signal to the dispensers (which were loaded with arrows.) Then, bam! bam! bam! The arrows would come flying toward the mobs. Pretty smart, huh?

After I stocked the dispensers with arrows, I went over to Alex to see how she was doing. Alex had long ginger hair and was wearing her usual green top with a utility belt. "Hey, Steve! How're the defences going?" she asked. Alex was pretty cheerful despite the circumstances; her father, Dave, was kidnapped by Herobrine and taken to the End dimension. We had two weeks to rescue him, but we needed to protect the village first.

"Pretty good!"

"Why are you so happy today?" I asked. I certainly wasn't feeling my best (having been targeted by a dangerous witch.) "Oh, you know, just having a goal to work towards. It was quite boring down in the dungeons!" she exclaimed brightly. "want to see my trap?" There was a pressure plate, so I assumed it had something to do with TNT. "Sure!" I replied. The more defences, the better.

Alex threw a rock at the pressure plate, which was actually placed on loose sand. The sand gave away and the activator would have fallen into an inescapable pit of lava. "Wow!" I said. It was a pretty cool trap, alright! A second later, Jay ran over. "Hey, Steve! Want to see my trap?" he asked. Since Jay was good with Redstone, I was sure he would have made something impressive.

"Sure!" I replied as he took me to the edge of the village. All I could see was a lever and a row of cobblestone blocks. "Go ahead and pull the lever!" he called. I yanked the lever down, and the cobblestone blocks were pushed up by pistons. Cool! Basically, it's a wall. I'll add more cobblestone then it will be massive!" Jay said. "there is no way the witch will beat us!"

It was now evening. All the defences were ready, and the villagers were equipped with iron axes. I had an iron chest plate, a shield, and a sword. We were ready to fight. Before long, the witch arrived with her hoard of mobs. She was wearing the same hat that she had in the jungle. She pointed at the village, and the mobs emerged from the trees. Skeletons, creepers, zombies, drowned, phantoms, husks, and even a few charged creepers stood before me.

They slowly began to move towards me. Everyone else was hidden to take the witch by surprise.

I pulled down on the lever. A colossal wall separated the hundreds of mobs. The few that were on our side looked terrified, which is weird because they were supposed to terrify us.

The rest of the party emerged from their hiding places. Alex, with a trident, Jay with a crossbow, and fifty strong villagers with axes (some of them were too old or young to battle). We charged toward the mobs and fought. This was it. The battle against the witch had resumed. I slashed and sliced through the mobs. The arrow dispensers caused dozens of them to fall at my feet. A charged creeper, three skeletons, five zombies, and a husk fell into Alex's lava pit. The villagers had also constructed an underground TNT system. I bet you can guess what happened next. Yep. BOOM!

Just as I thought we were winning, something terrible happened. An absolutely huge zombie grew from nowhere. It was taller than the 150-block wall. It must have been one of the witch's various potions that had caused this.

A few villagers screamed and ran towards their houses. The zombie punched through Jay's wall. The wall crumbled as the sheer force of the punch was just too much. More mobs poured in through the debris. We were outnumbered 10 to 1. If you think that's enough, all of our warriors abandoned the battle. Including Jay and Alex.

I saw the witch's purple eyes glare at me through the swarm of mobs. At first, it seemed that the mobs were targeting me, but the witch probably wanted to deal with me

personally, so she sent them charging through into the village. I stood and waited as the mobs rushed by.
I wanted to help everyone back there, but I had my own battle to fight. I turned to face the witch. "Well, well. Who do we have here?" she asked sweetly. "I won't let you attack our village." I retorted coldly.

The witch laughed. "Oh really?" She threw a bright orange potion at me, which I deflected with my shield. I attacked with my sword, but the witch was actually quite strong. She caught the blade under her arm and sent a kick at me. I stumbled back. The witch dropped a splash potion on the ground. The vial shattered, and my eyes stung as smoke rose up into the air. I felt a couple of sharp blows to the head before I collapsed like a bridge with shoddy construction. As quick as a flash, the witch bound me in tight vines which crept around my hands and feet. I was forced to drop my weapons. I was unarmed.

I called for help but everyone had run inside, apart from Alex and Jay, who were rounding up stray villagers. Meanwhile, the mobs were destroying the village. They trampled on our priceless crops, which were so hard to grow. The creepers exploded near houses. Skeletons fired arrows at our livestock. But the biggest danger was the giant zombie.
It was smashing the cottages with its gargantuan fist and stomping on villagers. I could just watch helplessly. I kicked and struggled, but I just could not break out of the vines. The witch was just standing there cackling. "Let me go!" I bellowed, but the witch ignored me.

After she had enough fun watching the village get destroyed, she called her army back. I saw Jay calling after me, but he was too far away.

His crossbow was loaded, but he knew that if he shot at the witch, he might hit me. Alex was nowhere to be seen. At least, that's what I thought.

I twisted around, and there she was, hiding behind a large rock. Alex obviously thought that she could get close enough to free me. I shook my head, but she didn't listen. It didn't matter, though. As soon as she got close to me, Alex bounced back. Ughh. A force field How was that even possible?

Luckily, the witch didn't seem to notice Alex. By now the mobs had poured back inside the forest. Alex doubled up behind the rock, hoping not to be seen. As for me, the wicked witch ordered her mobs to carry me back to the swamps. There was no point in struggling. I could only escape when I reached the hut. The forest was dark and gloomy at night.

Strips of moonlight shone through the gaps in the leaves and branches, illuminating the witch's face. I tried to keep track of where we were going, but I was too tired. My eyelids felt like lead and I didn't have the energy to move a muscle. I decided to close my eyes for just one second...

I awoke about six hours later. It was nearly dawn. The group of zombies that had been carrying me were now wearing leather caps to protect themselves from the sunlight. I noticed we were still in the forest, which meant the witch had changed the location of her base.

And boy, was it impressive! We emerged into a large area that had been cleared of trees. It was swarming with mobs, left, right, and centre.

There were several lookout towers that were constructed of wood and cobblestone. A skeleton manned each of these. There was also a farm that grew Nether warts. They were useful in potions. The zombies laboured under the scorching sun, ripping weeds out of the soil. The witch also built herself a modified hut. It was several stories high, guarded by creepers that were tethered to fences. A murky pond accommodated the drowned, who didn't need to wear caps since they were in the water.

However, every single mob had that same hypnotised look: their eyes were purple. As I was taking all this in, a stray gave me a rough push in the back. I was scared because I didn't know what the witch wanted from me and what she was going to do to me.

The evil witch came to stand next to me. She cackled smugly. "What do you think of your new home?" the witch asked me. A new home? "I -I don't know what you mean. I have only one home, and that is Daint." I said. The witch continued watching her zombies work.

She sighed. Then she said, in a colder tone, "You don't get it, do you?" I will control your mind and you will become my greatest soldier. Then we shall finally take over the world side by side! Hahaha!" I was horrified. I didn't underestimate the witch because if she could command an army of hostile mobs, she could control me. "You can't. And you won't." I replied. There was no way I was going to turn on my friends back home.

"And how exactly do you plan to stop me?" she asked, with an arrogant look on her warty face. "Um, let's see," I said out loud. "I'll-" The witch cut me off abruptly (good thing she did, because I didn't know what I was going to say next).

"That's what I thought," she said simply. "Guards, take him away!" She beckoned to a few vicious-looking zombies in iron chest plates. They shoved me up the witch's front porch and into her hut. I have to say, it was quite impressive-at least for an evil witch. On her first floor, she had item frames bearing empty glass bottles. A black cat lay lazily on a rug that looked like it was made in the Victorian era.

A couple of plants filled the edges of the room. There was a fireplace in front of the rug- it was burning nicely. It was all quite homely if you didn't consider the fact that a warty old witch lived here. The next two floors weren't half as nice. The second floor was filled with steaming cauldrons and hissing brewing stands. The smell nearly made me vomit. Other than the tools, there was nothing else.

The zombies hauled me up to the third floor. As soon as I entered, I knew I was in big trouble. The floor was scattered with monster spawners. Most of these made creepers. The witch ordered her mobs to take me to the far end of the room. There, she made more vines appear to bind themselves around me. The vines were plastered to the wall and were covered with jagged thorns.

They dug into me, but that was the least of my worries. The witch was approaching me with a bottle in her hand. It was jet black and smelled putrid.

She ordered me to open my mouth, but I refused. I thought this would infuriate her just enough to drop the potion. It was an illogical, absurd thought, but that was all I had in the name of hope. Unfortunately, the witch just smirked and pinched my nose. I didn't dare to open my mouth for air, but I couldn't bear it. I gasped. The witch poured the potion down my throat.

I felt exhausted. I sank to my knees and grabbed my head. It was a thousand times worse than a normal headache. Then everything went pitch black. I felt something slam into me and I opened my eyes. But I wasn't in the hut. I was in a dark room.

Squinting, I watched the obscure figure at the other end of the room. It was the witch. Arms folded, she walked towards me slowly. Her eyes were glowing purple once more. Then, without warning, I stood up. I couldn't control myself. My head was telling me to not listen to the witch, but my body had other ideas. It was like the witch was controlling my body, not my mind. I was now doing everything the witch wanted me to do. Then I saw them. Alex and Jay were shouting at me, but I couldn't hear what they were saying. I was now completely controlled by the witch.

I tried to draw my sword out to attack the witch, but I couldn't. My hand wouldn't allow me to. The scene dissolved again as I stood at the banks of a lake. It was crystal clear and I could see my reflection. Everything was normal apart from my eyes. They were also purple. Then Alex and Jay's reflections replaced mine. They were still shouting, but it was of no use.

Then everything started disappearing in the black, curling mist. I woke again once more, still spooked by everything I had seen. I was back in the room with monster spawners. A creeper had just appeared from a spawner. I thought I was done for, being tied to the wall, but the creeper disregarded me with a shake of its head. I realised that I was one of them now. A zombie cut me free with a stone sword. I tried to attack, but my limbs locked up. Instead, they took me down the stairs.

I tried to break out again, but I knew there was just no way to do so. By now, I had reached the door. I stepped outside where the witch was. She had gathered an army; she was about to start her speech.

"The time has come, my loyal warriors, to attack. For centuries, people have attacked our mobs. Now it is our turn. Are you with me?" The mobs raised their arms. Well, It's not like they had a choice. I unwillingly raised mine as well. "Good. Now prepare to fight!" The witch finished. Every living thing there, apart from the witch, rushed towards the weapons shack. They were equipping themselves with all sorts of things, including chest plates, shields, boots, helmets, leggings, swords, tridents, and axes. They were serious. Before I say anything else, I am definitely not counting myself as 'they'. Even though I might do the same things as them, I would never be a mob. Nevertheless, I could still feel the witch's hypnotic powers getting stronger.

I no longer struggled as she ordered me around through telepathy. This was partly worrying, but I had bigger fish to fry. How was I going to stop the witch and keep my friends safe?

But the thing was, I didn't really care anymore. I was a servant of the witch. At the time, I didn't know that the witch was actually taking over my mind this time. Her powers got stronger the longer I was under her control. But I didn't have time to think about that now. The witch was handing out potions of strength. I recognised it from the witch's brewing stand a while back. I gulped my share down without hesitating. I had had one of these before- it was down in an underground cave while fighting Herobrine.

I suddenly felt a lot stronger. I unsheathed the cracked iron sword I had received. As a note, I'm pretty sure I was one hundred percent mind-controlled now. In some stories, I heard that victims subject to mind-controlling had no memory of what had happened. But I seemed to notice every little detail. The witch's potion must have been super-powerful.

I now knew that this is what the witch had been brewing: the ultimate potion. When we first met, I didn't think much of the witch. But time told me otherwise. She was nearly as powerful as Herobrine, if not at the same level. The witch broke my trail of thoughts, and I started moving towards the end of the forest, towards Daint. But everything came to a screeching halt. I heard the sound of footsteps from deep in the forest. It was an army of villagers led by Jay and Alex. But for some reason, I didn't feel happy to see them. Could the witch control my emotions?

I didn't have time to think. Without any of her smooth words, the witch sent us into battle. She had retreated into her hut.

The witch should have got herself some popcorn and watched the fight in her comfiest armchair as well.

I changed my tune when she threw a splash potion down from the window. It slowed a handful of villagers who were trying to reach the hut. On top of that, another zombie had transformed into a massive, hulking beast. He rampaged through everything in sight. As for me, I was battling it out with a few villagers. The potion had made me stronger, so I easily disarmed them and whacked them away with the hilt of my sword. I saw Alex and Jay bravely fighting their way to the hut. Then the witch spoke to me from inside my head. 'Get them,' she whispered.

I confronted my friends with my sword ready. "Steve!" Jay made his way forward, but I sent him flying back with a kick. "Um, are you okay?" Alex asked. But I wasn't listening. I was already charging at the pair. Alex parried my strike with her trident but didn't attack. She said, "Steve. Listen to me." I raised my sword, but Jay blocked the blow with his shield. With the determination of an angry iron golem, I swung the hilt of my sword round at his head.

He ducked and tackled me to the ground. I landed with a thud but pushed him off as I regained balance. All this time, I heard the witch's voice in my head: "Yes, yes! Keep attacking!" I tried to hit Alex with my sword, but she caught the blade in between her trident. With a deft flick, she sent my sword flying into the trees. I roared in rage. While I was distracted, Jay sneaked up behind me and tied me up to a tree. As I struggled, I saw Alex pulling out a golden potion from inside her backpack.

The moment I saw it, the witch was screaming, 'NO! Don't drink it!

I struggled against the biting ropes. I bellowed once more in anger when I found that I couldn't escape. Alex took the opportunity to shove the potion down me. At once, I felt loads better. The weight came off my shoulders that I didn't even know was there. I could see the pimply face of the witch shrinking and her cries dimming. Then everything dimmed away and I was left with just darkness.

When I came to, the battle was still raging. I was behind a large oak tree, hidden from view. Alex and Jay were pouring over me like bees to a can of soda. "Steve? Steve?" asked Alex urgently as she slapped me repeatedly.
Jay was about to pour a bucket of water over me when I replied, "I'm fine! I'm fine!"

Both Alex and Jay breathed a sigh of relief. "Thank goodness," Jay said. "we thought you were going to be like that forever!" Alex frowned. "I didn't. I knew that you would become the regular Steve that you are now. So, shall we repay the favour to the witch? "

"Let's do this," I said. "Jay, can you take care of the remaining mobs?" Even if we defeated the witch, the mobs would still be there.

"Sure!" he said. "get that witch!" Alex and I fought the mobs until we reached the hut. We ducked as a creeper blew the door open in an attempt to stop us.

The two of us sprinted into the house, climbing the stairs rapidly-oh. Was that a tripwire?

Whoomph! A wall of dispensers shot fire charges I dodged the blow, but Alex had been caught in the chest. Alex flew back and crash-landed into the scummy lake. Alex!" I screamed, but to no use. I couldn't see her in the opaque waters. I wanted to save Alex, but I needed to deal with the witch first. I ran up the final flight of stairs and came face to face with the witch herself. "Aaah, Steve, it seems like you have broken out of your little trance." Then her eyes turned steely grey and she brandished a fresh potion of strength. I swung my sword at her, but she ducked and kicked me to the floor. She made to grab another potion from her brewing stand, but I kicked the table and knocked the stand off.

It shattered, spilling green potion over the floor. Taking advantage of the witch's horror, I rammed my shield into her and she slammed into the glass window, which cracked slightly.

She got to her feet just as I struck out with my sword. She parried with a broken table leg and knocked the air out of me.

Gasping, I stood up, but the witch had flipped me into the table, which ended up as a pile of matchsticks. I tried to stand, but the pain in my stomach was too much. The witch then pulled out the dreaded black hypnosis potion. I closed my eyes, accepting my fate. The witch uncorked the bottle, about to use it one last time on me.

I certainly didn't want to be mind-controlled again, but there was nothing I could do. I thought of nothing apart from how I was never going to save Dave.

I owed him so much, but here I was, defeated. At least things weren't getting any worse now. The witch gave me her signature cackle, but her gleeful expression turned upside down in no time. The tip of a trident was jutting out of her velvety robes. And that trident was rather familiar. Speechless, I watched as the witch slumped down to the floor, lifeless. And there, standing in her place, was none other than Alex. She smiled and asked, "Do you need a hand?"
"So, how did you both find me?" I questioned Alex and Jay. "Simple." Jay said. "the abnormal amount of footprints in the middle of the forest."

We all laughed, and Shadow purred in my lap. We were back home in Daint. The rest of the mobs, who were supposedly fearless, had fled back into the forest, never to be seen again.

We had won the battle. Order was restored at our home. The Village Elder had come by earlier to congratulate me once again for saving the day. But it wasn't all me.

It was mostly the valiant villagers, the iron golem, and, above all, Jay and Alex. Without them, I probably wouldn't have been where I am now. Now there was only one thing left to do, and then our work would be done It would be the most dangerous of our adventures, but we could do anything together.

It was time to go to the End and stop Herobrine once and for all.

CHAPTER 5

The End

The towering obsidian pillars loomed over the archipelago. The small islands dotted around the mainland were floating over the endless void, illuminated by the end crystals perched atop the pillars. In the midst of the endstone chunk, Enderman teleported left, right, and centre. Time was not a thing in this world, as shown by how this unique environment had not changed since its unexplained appearance.

Perched upon a bedrock block was the Ender Dragon. The beast's razor-sharp fangs dripped with saliva, and dull grey scales jutted out of her muscled body. Its leathery wing's delicate bone structure allowed it to glide across the land with ease. Anybody foolish enough to challenge the monstrous creature would not be spared by the powerful purple fireballs she launched.

The land had been undisturbed for millennia. Until he came. Out of nowhere, a player emerged on an obsidian platform not far from the foreboding mainland. The player wore a hardy set of diamond armour over his casual light blue shirt and purple trousers. He could have been mistaken for a simple and adept player. But he was much more. For this clandestine figure was Herobrine. The all-powerful villain. He teleported across to the mainland and approached the dragon. It had never seen anything like Herobrine in the course of its long life.

The dragon, who was not to be mistaken as careless, eyed Herobrine, making sure he didn't make any moves towards the obsidian pillars that she relied on so much.

At last, Herobrine spoke in a clear and steady voice. "O, almighty God of Minecraft! I have come forth to warn you of a grave danger that is approaching. They are coming. The people of the Overworld seek your dimension. They come in search of the Earth-dweller which I bought here previously." He indicated a figure tied to the bedrock perch. "I believe that these people will come to this dimension in the very near future. I am gladly willing to help protect you and your world, but only for a price. Help me end these foul humans and we will rule the world side by side.

The Ender dragon considered what it had just heard. Unlike most animals, it understood English. The proud creature didn't exactly feel the need for protection, but there was something about Herobrine that made her obey his orders. She didn't sense anything wrong about this strange human - or was he?

Nor did she think that his abrupt appearance in her kingdom was off. Regardless, she roared her approval. Herobrine smirked, satisfied. It was child's play for him. Now let Steve and his puny friends try to save Dave, he thought maliciously. The game was in the bag for him. He would be the ruler of the universe in no time.

Chapter 5.1

I woke to a sliver of sunlight that signalled early dawn. I checked the antique clock hanging on the wall. It was 6'O clock in the morning. Time to start the journey to the End. You see, Me, Alex and Jay need to save Dave (Alex's dad) from the End. Herobrine has kidnapped him and given us a very short time to rescue him.

After a contradictory discussion with my friends and many hours of reading up about the End, we decided that today was as good as any day to begin our ultimate adventure. I rolled out of bed and woke Jay and Alex, who were slumbering in their rooms. They didn't have time to build their own houses, but after a bit of expanding my house, there wasn't really a need. Anyway, luxuries would have to wait.

I woke up Alex and Jay, who were both very groggy. "C'mon guys, let's get to the armoury." After a quick bite for breakfast, we headed to the armoury. Nobody was awake yet, so there wasn't a sound as we walked past the thatched houses. I averted my gaze from the colossal stone wall that had partially crumbled. It brought back the memory of what happened only a few days ago. A massive zombie who was in the witch's army had punched through the wall and created an entry for all the mobs who were under the command of the witch. But I was able to defeat her with a little (cough, cough) help from my friends. We soon reached the armoury, and I twisted the brass knob, which led to the weapons and armour inside. There was every kind of armour, from leather to diamond.

"Alright guys, get suited up!" I said. We decided to have a full diamond armour set, which meant that the armoury would be pretty much empty after we left but we had no choice. We were facing advanced mobs and villains like Herobrine, so we needed advanced armour. We got a diamond sword each and a pickaxe. We also grabbed a few golden apples before we checked out some ranged weapons. I and Alex took a regular bow each, which would be good for shooting down the Ender Dragon.

Jay chose a crossbow because he preferred weapons that did more damage, not load quicker. Alex also grabbed her signature weapon, a trident. We loaded up with a few other tools like axes and spyglasses before we headed to the enchantment section. The enchantment section had anvils, enchantment tables, bookshelves, and chests filled with lapis lazuli. I enchanted my chest plate with protection III. It was a pretty powerful enchantment, but I had enough experience. Plus, I enchanted my sword with fire aspect I, which would set anything I hit on fire. Apart from the Ender Dragon unfortunately. Alex enchanted her trident with loyalty II and her diamond helmet with blast protection.

Jay enchanted his crossbow with multishot and his boots with feather falling. That would come in handy if the Ender Dragon decided to knock him off the obsidian towers! After we enchanted our gear, we grabbed some other useful items like a bucket, which would help us make a Nether portal; some bread, to keep our stomachs full, a shield each, and a bed, which, believe it or not, explodes in the End and Nether if a player tried to sleep in it!

After half an hour of foraging for helpful items, we started our epic journey. But before we left, we needed to say goodbye to the village elder. I knocked on the door and it swung open to reveal the elder who was still in his pyjamas. "Hello, you three! Are you all ready? "We all nodded. "Good. I hope to see you soon. Please be careful! " "Don't worry! We'll be just fine! "Jay said. The village elder nodded and said," "Well, good luck. Oh, and also bring back an Ender dragon head from the End ships. It would look quite nice above my door." he joked. We all laughed as I went back to my house to say goodbye to Shadow, my pet ocelot.

I stroked her head while she mewed. I did consider taking Shadow along, but I couldn't risk her getting hurt. She was only a small cat, after all. I took one final look at Daint before we walked away from the village and into the unknown. "Alright. We need to find a lava pool to make a Nether portal." Alex said. "then from there, we can get blaze rods from the Nether fortress you were telling us about." I bit my lip. I wasn't worried about going into the Nether since I had been there before, but there was a catch. The Wither was still there. A while ago, our village was attacked by the Wither. I banished it in the Nether because A: It was too powerful to actually destroy and B: I had no intention of ever going back to the Nether. Jay patted me on the shoulder and said, "Don't worry. "The Wither can't be hanging around there for a year." I hoped Jay was right. We continued looking around a bit, but our search was fruitless. How hard was it to find a lava pool? We walked for a couple of hours until we reached the desert. The scorching sun beat down on my neck and dead shrubs crunched beneath our boots. This was hopeless.

I thought about going back to the ruined Nether portal in the forest back home, but I remembered that it had been mined down to nothingness. We decided to make camp for the night as the beautiful orange sunset shone down from above. Alex mined some wood while Jay and I built a small cabin. We took the beds that we collected out of our inventories and slept for the night.

***

Groan. Huh? Was that a husk? It was early in the morning: Day 2 of our adventure. I swung open the door and found three repulsive husks banging on our door. They were covered in musty bandages and had grey, scabbed skin. The husks were basically mummified zombies who could survive during the day. I unsheathed my sword and put the husks out of their misery.

All the commotion had woken up Alex and Jay. "What's going on?" Alex asked. I replied, "Just husks," I replied. Jay climbed out of his bed and yawned, "We should get a move on." We packed up our things and hit the road. Then I spotted something out of the corner of my eye. A sandstone structure jutted out from the dunes- was it a desert temple? I pointed it out to Jay and Alex, who literally dragged me to the temple before I could ask them what it was. "Finding a desert temple that's so cool!" remarked Alex, entering the dark building. Jay said, "I bet there's some good loot!" The three of us crept into the temple, cautious of traps. Soon, we came to a chequered pattern of tiles on the floor. This was where the loot probably was.

I pulled out my iron pickaxe and mined down. Alex and Jay stayed where they were so they could send a rope down to pull me up.

As I landed, I noticed a stone pressure plate on the floor covering TNT. I mined the plate and the TNT. It would come in handy later. Then I released the clasps on the four chests and rummaged through the loot. Saddles, bones, gunpowder, string and diamonds! I collected the three diamonds from the chest. We could make a diamond pickaxe out of this!

There were also some iron and gold ingots, so I pocketed them as well. I called up to Alex and Jay, and they reeled me in with a fishing rod. I shared the spoils with them, and we walked out of the temple discussing the loot. They would surely help us on our quest!

* * *

Night had fallen once again. Tonight, we took shelter in a small cave. Everything was pitch black. I lit some torches up and stared into the darkness. There were a few husks and creepers roàming around, but I doubted they could see us. Then I saw a bright light coming from the floor about a hundred feet away. I pulled out my spyglass and zoomed in. It was a lava pool! "Guys, come here!" I found a lava pool! "I was super excited because we had just made a huge step forwards.
Alex gasped, surprised. "Let's go!" We ran from our base, taking cover from the mobs in the darkness. The heat from the lava made me sweat. The pool was bubbling ferociously as the lava sloshed around. Jay rubbed his hands together.

"Alright. We can make a Nether portal with the bucket of water." First, we dug a 2 by 2 hole to make an infinite water source. Then, we carefully poured bucketfuls of water into the lava. The lava sizzled when touched by the water and morphed into a block of obsidian. Yes! This was working! Bit by bit, we built up the portal. But as Alex turned to face the incomplete portal, she accidentally kicked the bucket of water into the lava.

We all stared as the precious substance hardened into obsidian. There was no lava left. Alex gasped. "I am so sorry!" Jay, who seemed horrified, said, "It- it's ok, Steve can make a diamond pickaxe from the diamonds we found earlier, right?"

I nodded before we got to work. Jay placed down a crafting table, and Alex placed down two sticks and all three diamonds. I held the final product up to examine. It looked like it could break all the obsidian within a minute. It turned out that it took no less than twenty minutes to chip away all the obsidian. Wiping my sweaty brow, I said, "We can fill in the rest of the portal now." That took no time compared to how long it took to break the obsidian. Soon, we had a fully functional portal. "Come on, guys, let's go." Alex said, determined. Jay and I stepped in after her. Everything swirled around in a blur of purple before I stepped out into the Nether.
I emerged out onto a ledge above a lava lake. "Uhh, guys, look up!" said Jay urgently. A Ghast was looming above us. The creature sent fireball after fireball at us. Most of them missed, flying into the lava. The Ghast shrieked angrily and shot a fireball with deadly accuracy We dived aside as the fireball hit collided with the ground. BOOM!

Netherrack blocks flew everywhere. Thick smoke stung my eyes and I couldn't see a thing. Once the smoke had cleared I couldn't see Jay of Alex anywhere. They had either ran to safety without me or got blown into the lava. I could hear shouts not too far away. I tried to call out, but the smoke made me cough.

I couldn't see it, so I pulled my sword out for protection. I raised my shield above my face. The Ghast would strike at any moment. The smoke was clearing, so I would have a better view of the Ghast. It then screamed again from behind me as I whipped around. The Ghast fired another fireball at me as I deflected it with my sword. It flew above its head and exploded on a group of hoglins. Suddenly, the Ghast launched three fireballs at me simultaneously. One skimmed my shoulder, I sent the other straight back at the Ghast but the last one slammed into me. I just had time to see the Ghast float to the floor before the fireball collided with me and burst into a dome of fire.

Things were a bit confusing after that. There was more smoke and Netherrack blocks. I heard a loud explosion more powerful than the last during the fireball impact. Then I felt a sharp pain in my stomach where the fireball had hit. I didn't know what happened next. I ended up lying on the banks of the river for who knows how many hours later. I stood up, spitting dirt out of my mouth.
A pile of gunpowder was left in place of the Ghast. That was way too close! I gathered up my items and travelled through a narrow tunnel. I couldn't find my bow, so I guessed it had fallen into the lava lake. The tunnel was cool compared to the rest of the Nether but it was still probably thirty degrees in there.

I heard magma cubes bouncing around in the distance. I needed to find Alex and Jay. I hoped that they were safe. But first I had to get to the fortress. I had no idea where it was though, so I pulled out my compass. Little did I know, compasses had no effect in the Nether. The dial was spinning around wildly, like it was broken. I sighed and slipped it back into my pocket. I was on my own here; the deepest place in the world. Wait, I'm not even in my world! I found some gold, but I didn't have time for a nice mining trip right now. I walked through the tunnel for another hour before I saw light at the end of the tunnel.

I quickened my pace and soon reached the end of the tunnel. I emerged into a familiar cavern. It had streams of lava running down from the ceiling and crimson trees crowding a small patch of land. But the strange thing was that there were no mobs. It had been a mob holiday destination the last time I had come here... And there, easily noticeable on the top of a cliff, was the Nether Fortress. It was not in good condition; the Wither had blown many of the rooms right open. There was lots of debris at the foot of the fortress. Still, I couldn't believe that I had found it!

Remembering what had happened here so long ago, I pulled my diamond sword out. I jumped off the ledge I was standing on and slowly crept towards the foreboding fortress. There were large holes in the ground made by the Wither when it was chasing me. It had been absolutely terrifying!

But I couldn't see nor hear the Wither. Where had it gone? Then I saw a three-headed shadow behind me. The Wither had been planning and ambush. I turned around to face it. Its white eyes were glowing strangely.

It was hovering in mid-air, as if considering whether to attack me or not. Then there was an even bigger surprise. Herobrine emerged from the shadows. He smirked unpleasantly at me. His eyes were just like the Wither's: a glowing white. It was unnerving how Herobrine resembled me so closely.

"Steve." he began coldly. "I will not bother to fight you today." Herobrine clicked his fingers and metal chains rose from the ground and slowly wrapped themselves around me. I struggled at them as the cold metal bit into my skin. Herobrine walked towards me and grabbed hold of my shirt. Then everything disappeared in a flash of blinding white and I re-emerged inside the fortress. He had teleportation powers!

Herobrine released me from my chains and continued talking. "I could finish you now, but I prefer you being trapped in an inescapable room." Such fun! Now give me all your tools! "I knew there was no point in arguing, so I reluctantly gave him my pickaxe, axe, spyglass, compass, golden apples, and my spare iron sword. I had slipped my diamond sword into my belt behind me. I hoped Herobrine hadn't noticed. Though for some reason, I thought Herobrine knew a lot more than he let on. "Now follow me!" I dragged myself out of the room. I didn't know how this was going to end. At least I still had my armour. Herobrine had come to a stop. "Get in!" he shouted. Herobrine pushed me into the small room. It was probably the tiniest room in the entire fortress! It was practically pitch-black inside and the only source of light came from the window, which had wooden fencing acting as bars. I could see a small spider scuttling around the dusty floor.

It was basically a prison cell. I sat down and leaned against the wall. I hoped Jay and Alex would find the fortress and rescue me. Then I remembered that I had a flint and steel in my shirt pocket. I could burn away the fence! I was so happy that I could have danced for joy. I did notice that the fences were made from wood, not Nether bricks. But then again, the Wither had probably destroyed the original fencing, which was probably why the fences were made of wood. Herobrine must have missed out that small detail! I got to work scraping the steel rod against the flint. Soon, the fence had burned away, and there was a hole just big enough for me to squeeze through. Yes!

I cautiously climbed out of the window, careful not to make any noise when the door opened. It was Herobrine. "Hmm? What's going on?" Herobrine roared in a rage and bellowed something. I heard a loud shriek not far away. I ducked out of Herobrine's sight and started to block across yet another lava lake. The Wither's howls sounded closer, so I started blocking quicker. I reached the other side of the cliff and started running. But I came to an abrupt halt as the Wither stood before me. The thing that was even crazier was that Herobrine was riding it.

He glared at me before motioning the Wither to attack. The Wither sent skull after skull at me, each exploding viciously. I raised my shield to block each skull, which blew up with such a force that I was thrown back into the gap which I had just bridged across. I screamed as I tumbled through the air. But I guess it was my lucky day because I had just managed to hold onto the edge of the bridge. I felt my fingers slipping, so I made a huge effort to pull myself up.

Gasping for air, I took a breather right on the middle of the bridge. Well, that was a mistake! The Wither shot a blue skull directly at me.

The Wither fired another skull at me and gave me the Wither efffect. The middle section of the bridge exploded, and I was falling towards the lava once more. There was no hope this time. The lava was drawing closer and closer. I shut my eyes. Then I felt strong hands grab onto me. There was a pop, which signified teleportation. Had Herobrine had a change of heart and decided to save me? It turned out it wasn't Herobrine. I opened my eyes to find Lofty the Enderman crouching down beside me. I couldn't believe my eyes. Lofty?

I had made friends with him in the Nether when he needed my help with some Ender pearl thieves! And here he was, saving me from doom. "Th-thanks." I managed. Lofty vvooped and looked around. We had teleported just outside the fortress, inside the small portion of the crimson forest. I explained my predicament to Lofty. Since he was an Enderman, he could use telepathy. Lofty said that he would distract the Wither while I collected blaze rods. After I had done that, we would find Alex and Jay and get out of the Nether. What could go wrong?

First, Lofty and I teleported right below the fortress. Lofty would have to leave me here because it was too risky to teleport straight into the structure where Herobrine was sure to be waiting. He chirped his goodbyes and teleported away. I stared up at the sheer cliff face. How was I going to climb that? Unless... I started gathering up as much Netherrack as possible. I was going to block it up.

I carefully pillared my way into the fortress. Time to change to full ninja mode, I thought. Quietly but quickly, I set off in search of the blaze spawner.

Climbing a stairwell, running down a corridor, exploring a dark room... where was that spawner? I tried to cast my mind back to when I had seen a glimpse of the blaze spawner when I had first been in this place.

But it was of no use- too much had happened since then for my brain to remember. The only option was to keep looking. It turned out that I was wrong about there not being any mobs. I found a few Wither skeletons every few paces along my search. That meant that things took twice as long as they should because there wasn't much searching that I could do with a dozen Wither skeletons swarming me. I finally fought off what was hopefully the last group of skeletons before I found the spawner.

It was inside a dark, decrepit room hidden away in the depths of the fortress. The flames from the spawner illuminated the room, which was solely dedicated to a single blaze spawner. I didn't see any blazes anywhere. I watched the needle on my watch spin around like a football in mid-air. Of course, I knew that the time displayed wasn't accurate because watches and compasses are basically pieces of useless scrap metal in the Nether. After about ten minutes of waiting, the first blaze rose from the spawner.
It was actually quite a small creature. Its blocky body was surrounded by spinning rods that circulated around it. These were the blaze rods I needed. Apart from literally being fire, blazes could shoot fireballs like the Ghast but as they didn't fly so high, I was able to take them out with my

diamond sword pretty easily. Unfortunately, the fire aspect enchantment didn't do anything on the blaze since it was already on fire.

Still, I got the rod. It was smoking and burned my hand as I tried to pick it up. Using my shield, I defeated a few more blazes and collected their rods. Now I had everything I needed. As I turned to leave, I heard loud explosions and angry shouts in the distance. Lofty! He needed my help. I followed the sound of the explosions and soon reached the scene of battle. Alex, Jay, and Lofty were taking on an army of Wither skeletons, the Wither itself, and Herobrine! I could celebrate finding them later. They needed my help.

I pulled out my sword and rushed straight into the action. Alex and Jay didn't pay any attention to me because they were battling hard: Alex with her trident and Jay with his sword. I fought through the Wither skeletons and proceeded towards Herobrine and the Wither. Herobrine ordered the Wither to attack. But this time he was serious about it. The Wither's immensely powerful blue skulls left a ringing noise in my ears as they exploded around me. The Wither was one rapid shooter! I couldn't get close as the explosions pushed me back. After getting blasted back into a tower wall for the third time, I realised that we didn't have to fight. I had the blaze rods, so all we had to do was escape. Then I had an idea. I pulled Jay aside from the battle and asked him to lend me his crossbow. "Why?" Jay asked. "Don't you already have a bow?" I shook my head. Jay handed me his crossbow. I pulled out an arrow from my inventory and dipped it into the lava.

It came out with its end smouldered. The sharp tip was melted into a blunt lump of metal, but I didn't care. This was all I needed. I loaded the arrow into the crossbow and fired a clean shot at the Wither. As the arrow flew through the air, it caught on fire and struck the Wither square in the head (or shall I say heads).

Now things were getting crazy. The Wither flew around everywhere frantically shooting skulls while shrieking loud enough to make someone deaf at the same time. "Guys, come on. We have to go!" I shouted over the sound of explosions.

We all linked our arms together as Lofty teleported to the portal. But the danger didn't stop there. Herobrine teleported in front of us, blocking the path towards the portal. "You will not escape." he said curtly. Herobrine clicked his fingers and chains appeared from the ground like giant worms. I moved out of their grasp and went for the portal. Herobrine reached his arm up to the bedrock ceiling, and a second later, a shower of arrows fell from the sky. (well, there wasn't a sky, but you know what I mean.) I took cover under my shield. Herobrine had some crazy powers! Alex threw her trident at him, but he teleported away and the trident flew through the portal.

But since Alex's trident was enchanted, it flew straight out of the portal and back into her hands. Then Herobrine flew up and levitated ten feet in the air. He pointed his arm at the portal, and it shook slowly. A second later, it burst into shards of obsidian. Herobrine destroyed the portal! Jay shouted, "RUN!" We fled, leaving Herobrine behind. As I ran, I could hear loud explosions coming from behind me.

It looked like the Wither was back. BOOM! I was thrown forward onto the ground. I had been hit. I slowly crawled forward. "Help," I called coarsely. Jay lumbered back to me and picked me up in a fireman's lift. We continued to run until we caught up to the others. Alex and Lofty had blocked themselves into a small hill. Jay leaped in with me just as Alex put down the final block. It was pitch black. Jay set me down and lit a torch. "What happened?" asked Alex. Lofty also vvooped worryingly.

"The Wither," said Jay simply. "here, Steve, eat this." He handed me a golden apple. I quickly ate it and felt much better. However, I would have been a goner had it not been for all my armour. I sat up. "What now? "There's no way to escape the Nether for us." asked Alex. We sat in silence as we thought about how to escape without a portal. After pondering for a good five minutes, I had an idea. It was so simple that I couldn't believe that I hadn't thought of it before now. "Lofty, can you teleport us out of the Nether?"

Lofty tilted his head curiously. A second later, an answer flashed inside my mind. 'I can, but it would zap me of all my energy.' I stared sadly at the ground. I guess we wouldn't be teleporting through dimensions any time soon. Then Lofty said, 'Let's go. Just hold on tight.' My eyes widened. "Are you sure?" I asked. It wasn't worth exhausting him like that. Lofty nodded. Alex and Jay stood up and held onto Lofty's skinny, black arm. But as I got up, I heard a terrifying wail from outside.

The Wither! It had found us. I linked arms with Lofty and the four of us teleported just as the Wither blew our shelter to smithereens.

Gasping for air, we lay in a crumpled pile back in the desert. Thanks to a combination of teleportation powers and luck, we made it out alive. I breathed a sigh of relief. That had been way too close. Putting the blaze rods in my inventory, I settled down for a good night's sleep. The next morning, I awoke to some loud snoring. Scratching my head, I saw Lofty nestled in a bed. He was still out from teleporting us to the Overworld.

Jay and Alex came to stand beside me. "It was thanks to him that we got out safely." said Jay. Alex raised an eyebrow and pointed at our singed clothes, cracked armour, and the many cuts and bruises we had obtained. Jay laughed and said, "Ok, more or less!" By now, Lofty had woken up. He sat up in his bed. He looked very tired. All we had to do now was get Ender pearls to craft with the blaze powder that I had turned the rods into.

The problem was that we needed to hunt down Enderman for their pearls. I knew Lofty wouldn't take it very well, so I asked if he had any Ender pearls that we could use. Lofty handed them over without question. He was probably too tired to really care. I crafted the blaze powder and the Ender pearls together to make the eyes of Ender. We rested up for the remainder of the day, collecting wood and chatting. Lofty needed to be at full health for him to come with us to the stronghold.

The sun was setting when we decided to go. This was the final leg of our journey. I grabbed an eye of Ender tightly and threw it into the air. It floated a few metres East before falling to the ground. "That way." I pointed East. We walked in that direction for a couple of minutes before I threw another eye. This one was veering slightly to the left. We changed course and followed that eye. That was how the night went on. Throwing little objects into the air and following their trail. This was even worse than finding the lava pool. We trekked across the land all night. I even asked Lofty if he knew where the portal was, but Lofty said he didn't because he had no need for them, being able to teleport wherever he liked. I sighed. This was going to be hard.

We walked through the desert, the jungle, the tundra, forests, and every other biome imaginable. After an entire night of walking, we reached the ocean. Cold, wet and hungry, we weren't too fond of the prospect of crossing the freezing waters.

I lazily threw another eye. But this time, something different happened. The eye of Ender went straight down into the water. Was this it? Full of adrenaline, me, Alex, and Jay dived into the water. Lofty said that he would catch up with us later because he couldn't touch the water being an Enderman. I didn't even care that the water chilled me to the bone because we might have found the stronghold!
After all that we had been through, I was almost certain that this was it. We excitedly dug down, coming up occasionally for air. After making sure we had dug down deep enough, Alex blocked off all the water. Next, we set down the TNT, which I had gotten from the desert temple. Standing a good few metres away, we lit the explosives. Before we knew it, the roof of one of the rooms had been blown wide open. We lowered ourselves down and stared around in awe. We were in!

The mossy cobblestone bricks built up the dingy tunnels and dim torches lit up the main room. But my initial joy soon faded away. The stronghold was more of a labyrinth than a place for the ultimate portal to the End. I decided that the easiest way was to split up. I searched room after room for the portal. It was nowhere to be seen. After half an hour of searching, we came up with nothing. I was feeling hopeless now. We were so close... "Hey, guys, do you hear that?" I strained my ears to listen out for any sounds. I could hear a soft hiss.

Then, without warning, a silverfish slithered up to us and began nipping on our boots. Alex kicked it away in disgust as we approached the spawner. Jay quickly disabled it with five torches. But Alex wasn't watching the spawner. She was standing at the top of a staircase. "Guys, I found the portal."

Jay and I ran up the stairs. Sure enough, there was the portal. It consisted of twelve end portal frames arranged in a three-by-three layout. We just stood there and marvelled at it for a minute. Finally, pulling myself together, I filled in the portal one by one, careful not to misplace any eyes. Soon, we had the portal to the End. I took a deep breath and jumped in. We had reached the End. It turned out that I was on some sort of obsidian platform floating above the void. A second later, Jay and Alex joined me. "Let's go." I said. The End was a beautiful place, yet stranger than anything I had seen before. The entire mainland consisted of endstone, a common block in the End. There were a few obsidian pillars with end crystals on top of them- they healed the Ender Dragon. Speaking of it, I spotted the black creature flapping about at least a hundred blocks in the air.

When I was little, I was told that the End was above the Overworld just as the Nether was below the Overworld. I had wanted to visit it ever since. And here I was. I blocked across to the mainland as Jay and Alex walked onto my little dirt bridge. The Ender dragon didn't seem to notice us, which was a good thing because we didn't want anything to do with it. We needed to find Dave. A second after we arrived on the mainland, Lofty greeted us. But instead of being happy to see us, he looked petrified.

I heard his voice in my head. It's a trap- Herobrine! Get out! On cue, Herobrine materialised in front of us, grinning wickedly. We all turned to face him. You have fallen straight into my trap. "This is the End for you, Steve." he said calmly. I had a brief flashback to when I had first met Herobrine. A cheerful, decent young man. Well, that's what I thought he was. Herobrine was corrupted by greed and revenge. The result of that was right in front of me.

"Dave will never leave the End, just like you." he snarled. Herobrine thrust his hand at the perch and the Ender dragon smoothly glided down on top of a bedrock perch where Dave was tied on. Alex gasped. Dave's look said, 'HELP ME!" He didn't look too good after being stuck in the End for so long. Anyways, what was Herobrine's thing with befriending boss mobs? The Ender dragon roared at us. As if Herobrine and the ultimate boss mob weren't enough! Apparently, Herobrine didn't have the power to summon the Wither through dimensions, which was a good thing. Me, Jay, Alex, and Lofty faced our rivals. The other Enderman also joined the fight (on our side, of course).

Before the battle started, I whispered to Alex, "Get Dave out." Me and Jay would handle Herobrine and the Ender dragon. Alex nodded gravely.

I was about to fight the biggest battle of my life. I tensed, gripping the hilt of my sword tight. We had to win. I closed my eyes for a moment, reopening them with hope. We would win. I sprinted forward into the last battle. The Enderman tossed blocks of endstone at the Ender dragon, who retaliated with purple fireballs, casting dangerous magic every few feet.

I decided to focus on the Ender Dragon before taking on Herobrine. I blocked up onto the first pillar and destroyed the first crystal. I turned around to see the Ender dragon flying straight at me. I tossed an Ender pearl straight at the next pillar, destroying it just like the first. But the Ender dragon was too quick for me this time. I was hit by one of its purple fireballs, being blasted off ninety blocks down. Pulling my water bucket out just in time, I performed a water bucket clutch. Ducking out of the way of the Ender Dragon's second fireball. I ran to the third tower, shooting the crystal down with some snowballs that I had gathered in the tundra. I thought the Ender dragon was coming back for another attack, but I saw Alex cutting Dave free with her sword. It was going for them. I sped across the landscape and protected Alex and Dave with my shield.

The dragon's bony wing ran across my shield, requiring all my effort to push it away.

I quickly built a dirt wall, which would buy Alex a little bit of time to cut Dave free. I darted out from behind the wall and focused on the crystals. Bam! Boom!

I teleported across from tower to tower, destroying crystal after crystal. But just as I was about to teleport to the last tower, a blur of blue tackled into me at light speed, both me and Herobrine ploughing into the ground. Rubbing my shoulder, I stood up to face Herobrine. He dropped to his feet, staring directly at me. A dark, black blade appeared in his hand. It looked like it was made of shadows. I pulled out my diamond sword, swinging it at Herobrine. He teleported away, and by the time I had worked out where he had gone, I was sent flying into one of the obsidian towers. Smash! I picked myself up.

Crouching low, I blocked the barrage of arrows that Herobrine had sent at me with my shield. Twang! I leaped at Herobrine with my sword, but he was too fast. He swerved out of my way, slicing at me with his blade. Slash! I was thrown back viciously. To my utmost horror, my precious shield had been sliced clean in half. What? How? I leaned on my sword to stand. I couldn't defeat him like this! Clutching my left arm, I advanced towards my nemesis. Herobrine stabbed his sword into the ground, and a loud crack followed. A deep line in the ground ran towards me, getting larger and larger. I rolled away just as the crack opened into a large hole, swallowing everything that stood near it. The line in the ground closed up. I finally got close enough to use my sword, but Herobrine parried with his sword, sending mine flying into the void.

While I watched my sword disappear, glinting brightly as it fell, Herobrine took the opportunity to punch me to the edge of the island. Ouch! I was only metres away from the void. Herobrine could easily knock me down there. Herobrine teleported in front of me.

He pointed his shadow sword at me. "Any last words?" he said. I lay there defeated, not bothering to answer back. Herobrine really had won... or so he thought. Just as Herobrine lifted his blade to deliver the final blow, Jay, who had just warped near us, leaped at him, tackling him into the void with himself. NO! I stared over the edge of the island where the two figures grew smaller, disappearing in the cavity below. Forever. I couldn't believe it. Both of them. Gone. At that exact moment, the Ender dragon roared behind me, circling Alex and Dave, who were cowering behind the dirt wall. I stood up shakily. Jay had saved me. I was going to make sure it didn't go in vain.

Gripping my second-to-last pearl, I threw it onto the tallest tower. BOOM! The last End crystal had been destroyed. Now I had to get down. I scanned around for any Ender man who could help. Unfortunately, almost all of them had teleported away in fear or had fallen to the Ender Dragon. With the exception of one. Lofty. He was still making an effort to defeat the Ender dragon, throwing blocks at it, but the beast didn't seem to notice. I only had one more choice. I pulled out my final pearl. I couldn't miss. Alex had placed a bed next to her in an attempt to blow the Ender dragon out of existence, but she couldn't do it with Dave so close, who had no armour whatsoever. I mouthed at Alex to make a dash with Dave as soon as I teleported. She gave me a thumbs up. I signalled 3, 2, 1 and BAM! The bed exploded. The Ender dragon roared in pain. I myself hadn't been spared by the blast, but I didn't really care at this point. Alex stayed close to her father, supporting me by distracting the Ender dragon with her bow and arrow. I planted a second bed down. It blew up, setting the bedrock perch on fire.

I rolled away from the flames and placed down my last bed. But I didn't need to activate it. The dragon flew down low and blasted a fireball at me.

I practically felt it singe of the hairs on my arm as it whizzed past me, hitting the bed instead. A massive explosion followed. I was blasted away, landing painfully next to Dave, who was watching the battle from a distance. The Ender dragon roared one final time before slowly disintegrating into a shower of experience which rained upon me. The Ender dragon was defeated. Herobrine had gone forever. We had saved Dave. We had well and truly won.

Epilogue

[1 year later]

"Hey, Alex, do you want to visit Lofty in the End City?" I asked my friend. It was a bright and sunny day in Daint. "Yeah, sure!" Alex replied. We strolled through the village together until we reached my house. It was decorated with many souvenirs from my past adventures. An Ender pearl, a blaze rod, a diamond chestplate, the handle of my shield, just things like that.

My pet ocelot, Shadow, was curled up on my bed. I stroked her absent-mindedly. There was something I needed to do. I strode out of my house, passing the village elder who was sitting on his favourite bench. "Hello, Steve!" He shouted. I waved back. I could see Dave inside his house, crafting himself an iron axe. I finally reached my destination after a long walk in the forest. I approached a golden plaque which was labelled Jay. A crossbow lay at its feet. I laid down a bunch of flowers in respect of what he had done for me.

Turning away from the plaque, I walked back to the village. It was nearly night now. I sauntered towards the lake and sat on the shore, thinking about all the adventures I had had. They were definitely enough for one lifetime!

I happily sat there, staring at the captivating sunset. It was the perfect ending to the perfect adventure!

TDS PUBLICATION HOUSE
(Regd. Under MSME)

Our Tagline is:

YOU WRITE, WE PUBLISHED

TDS Publication House Known as "The Dreamers Studio Publication House".

The company was founded in the year 2020 by Shubham Kumar and Khushi Priya. It is registered under MSME Act. The business is a Proprietorship firm. It was earlier in Bihar. It is now in Punjab.

A Publishing House with an aim to give a platform to aspiring writers. This initiative started with an online competition platform to help aspiring writers show their talent. Then we extended our services, We introduced Publishing House to our buddy writers.

To date, We have **published 130+ books** (Anthologies & Solo Author Books) in the **last 19 months** and **created best-selling books also.**

Looking for a simple way to Print & Publish Your Book!!

Let TDS Publication House manage your Printing & Publishing Stuff while you focus on doing what you do best, which means writing more Books.

Want to Publish Your Own Book at an Affordable Price?

Contact us Today

Mobile No: 628 397 1078
Mail us: tds.publicationhouse@gmail.com

Or

Follow us on Social Media Handles:

Instagram: @tds.publicationhouse
Facebook: @tds.publicationhouse
LinkedIn: @tds.publicationhouse
Twitter: @tdspublication